# SECRETS IN TIME

## ALISON STUART

Oportet Publishing

Secrets In Time

Text Copyright © 2013 by Alison Stuart

ISBN: 9780995434202

This edition: Oportet Publishing 2018

Cover Design: Fiona Jayde

Formatting: Ebony McKenna

Discover other titles by Alison Stuart at www.alisonstuart.com

PRAISE FOR SECRETS IN TIME

"...a piece of innovative romantic fiction which will probably please readers of fantasy romance, historical romance, contemporary romance and even medical romance. Highly recommended....." *Historical Romance Reviews*

"...I'm a major fan of all things time travel, and this story was a delight. Jessica's willingness to suspend disbelief and help Nathaniel learn about her world was wonderful, and Nathaniel's courtly ways were just what she needed to heal her heart after a disastrous relationship ended..." *Bitten by Books for ARE Café (an ARE Café Top Pick)*

"...Likable characters, a sensually satisfying romance, realistic scenes of battle, and a clever mish-mash of paranormal elements and time travel all combine to create a memorable and intriguing story. Add this to another feather in Alison Stuart's writing cap..." *Amazon Reviewer*

# IS LOVE ENOUGH TO OVERCOME TIME...?

England 1995: Dr. Jessica Shepherd's peaceful summer afternoon is shattered by the abrupt arrival of a wounded soldier claiming to be from the seventeenth century.

If he is to be believed, Nathaniel Preston has crossed three hundred years bringing with him the turmoil of civil war and a request for help that Jess can't ignore.

Falling in love with this dashing cavalier is destined to end in heartbreak as Jess discovers the price of his love is the knowledge that he will die in battle in just a few short days.

Can their love survive a bloody battle...and overcome time?

Time Travel Romance

# Secrets

# IN TIME

# ALISON STUART

*This book is dedicated to the memory of my father, Arthur. Still miss you, Dad.*

## ❦ I ❦

# OVER THE WALL

### CHESHAM, NORTHAMPTONSHIRE

*June third, 1645*

I WILL NOT DIE. *Not today, not like this.*

*The six horsemen on my heels and the pistol balls that sing through the air around my head give lie to my intention. I know I have been hit, but there will be time later for pain.*

*Now I just have to survive.*

*We told the household I had been summoned to Oxford. I had not planned on running into a patrol of the enemy. Several of the scoundrels were local men who recognized me.*

*They shot my horse from under me as I turned to flee and now I am on foot.*

*As I cut across the fields on the outskirts of the Chesham village, I can see the cottage ahead. Behind me I hear the thunder of hooves.*

*Alice screams in my head, 'The wall, Nathaniel. You must go over the wall.' I must put my trust in witches and pray that Alice is right.*

---

## *June third, 1995*

HE CAME HURTLING over the garden wall into my neat little garden, breaking the bright foxgloves and dahlias I had labored over for so long. His shoulders tensed as he crouched low, resting his head against the wall, his chest heaving from the exertion of running.

I jumped off the dilapidated garden lounger, pulling the ear pieces of my Walkman from my ears in my haste.

'You idiot. What the hell are you doing? Get off my garden bed.'

The man jumped to his feet, swiveling to face me. He looked down at the trampled flower bed and obligingly stepped out of it.

As a person who spends far too much of her life around military re-enactors, the period costume and the sword at his hip seemed quite normal and not at all alarming.

My brother, Alan, is an enthusiastic participant in the local military re- enactment group and the presence of seventeenth century warriors in my garden is not as unusual as one might think. The village of Chesham had been the site of some minor skirmish during the English Civil War and Alan and his re-enactors are frequently called on to perform some duty at the bridge, generally followed by a visit to the village pub with me trailing along behind them.

As the intruder and I faced each other across my immaculate lawn, it occurred to me, despite the dirt streaking his clean shaven face and sweat darkened auburn hair, this man was a definite improvement to Alan's usual hirsute and overweight companions.

'Are you a friend of Alan's?' I enquired, my anger dissipating. When he didn't respond I continued, 'Look, I've nothing against the Civil War Association, or whatever it is you belong to, but this is private property.'

The man glanced toward the lane and returned his gaze to me, looking me up and down in an appraising manner. His right eyebrow arched and a smile twitched at the corner of his mouth. He took a breath and executed the sort of courtly bow I would expect of someone dressed as a seventeenth century cavalier. Alan's friends did it all the time.

'Mistress, I crave your pardon. I did not wish to intrude in such an unseemly manner. Please... if you wish to cover your-self...' He waved a hand at my person and turned away, poking at the crushed dahlias with his booted foot as if he thought he could resurrect them.

I glanced down at my crop top and shorts, and saw nothing untoward in my choice of dress for a quiet afternoon sunbathing in my own garden on a rare, beautiful, English summer day.

I wondered if I should make a sprint for the front gate and summon help from my elderly, deaf neighbor.

'Look, whoever you are,' I said. 'This is my house and my garden. You're trespassing. Please leave...' I pointed to the neat, green painted gate.

He looked in the direction I indicated and inclined his head. 'As you wish, mistress. I apologize for the intrusion.'

He took a couple of steps and grimaced, his right hand going to his left sleeve. The sleeve had been ripped and a dark stain marred the blue cloth of his jacket. He looked down at his arm as if noticing it for the first time and the color drained from his face.

I knew that look. Even as I sprang to his assistance, he crumpled at the knees, falling face down on the grass.

My instinct as a doctor overcame my reservations and I knelt beside him. As I turned him over into the coma position, he groaned and his eyes flickered open.

'You're hurt,' I said, stating the obvious.

He sat up, running a hand through his thick, dark hair. 'It's only a scratch. I have no wish to trouble you, mistress, but if I could perhaps have something to drink? Then I will leave you in peace.'

I gestured to the kitchen door. 'Come inside. I'll get you some water and have a look at that arm. The weapons you guys wield must be full of rust.'

As he rose to his feet, his knees threatened to buckle again so I took his good arm and we made slow progress into the kitchen.

Inside my bright, newly renovated kitchen he stopped and took a step backwards. 'What manner of a place is this?'

I looked around the room. Despite its expensive, modern fit out, it should have been immediately recognizable.

'My kitchen,' I said, with an uncertain quaver to my voice.

'Kitchen? It's like no kitchen I've ever seen. Where is your fire?'

'In the lounge room. Now sit down.'

My guest slumped into the chair at the table. He looked completely out of place in the modern surroundings, his clothes heavy and cumbersome for the warm day.

I fetched my bag of medical supplies from the bathroom and returned to the kitchen, to find him sitting rigidly upright with his eyes screwed shut.

'What are you doing?' I asked.

He opened one eye and gave me a crooked smile. 'Are you a witch?'

I laughed. 'Witch? Hardly. Although Alan did suggest if I ever wanted to join the Association I would make the perfect witch. Do you know Alan Shepherd?'

He frowned and shook his head. 'I think not.'

'Strange. I thought you all knew each other. He's with...let me think, what do they call themselves? Mortlock's Regiment.'

The gray-green eyes widened. 'A scurvy roundhead!'

I shrugged. With a professor of seventeenth century history in the family, the distinction between scurvy roundheads and cavaliers was not lost on me.

'Quite possibly. It seems to be all about running around with dangerous weapons and drinking mates. Now let's get that jacket off.'

Easier said than done. Re-enactors pride themselves on authenticity. To get to the jacket, we first had to remove the sword hanging from its baldric and untie the heavy silken scarf he wore around his waist. Then the dark blue woolen jacket had to be unlaced. Years of working in hospitals had made me quite adept at removing clothing from comatose patients and I had him down to shirt sleeves without hurting the injured arm.

'There. That must feel better. Fancy wearing all that kit on a day like today. You must be truly mad. Now the shirt.'

He regarded me through narrowed eyes. 'Do you know what you are doing?'

'I'm a doctor,' I replied.

'A doctor? But you're a woman.'

'Last time I looked. Do you want me to look at that arm or not?'

The left sleeve of his shirt was stiff with drying blood but the material had not yet adhered to the wound. I removed the shirt without resorting to scissors, revealing a rather attractive, well muscled chest.

The man grimaced as he raised his left arm to inspect the damage.

I clucked my tongue and turned my attention from the fine pectoral muscles to the arm, inspecting the deep, nasty gash in the firm biceps. This guy worked out.

Apart from a grim tightening of his lips, my patient did not flinch as I cleaned around the wound.

It had been a long time since I had done a stint in ER, and my patients are normally under the age of eighteen, but I had served my time in an inner city London hospital and I recognized a bullet wound when I saw one. Something with a high velocity had winged him.

'What did this?' I enquired.

He held my gaze with his for a long moment before saying through clenched teeth, 'It's of no matter.'

I met his gaze and felt him willing me not to comment further. To be honest, I didn't want the hassle of reporting a gunshot wound and all the attendant paperwork. I would patch him up and send him on his way. The less I knew, the better.

'This cut should be stitched. When did you last have a tetanus shot?' I asked.

His eyes widened. 'I have never shot a tetanus in my life!' He paused, frowning. 'I'm not even sure I've seen one. Are they dangerous?'

I had to bite my lip to stop from laughing. 'An injection, you dolt. When did you have your last tetanus injection?'

His brow furrowed. 'I don't think I have ever had an...injection.'

I sighed. 'I don't think I'll ever understand you re-enactors. I've been to a few of Alan's musters and quite honestly it amazes me that more people don't get seriously hurt.' I paused in cleaning the wound and looked up. 'I only saw Alan last night and he didn't mention anything about a muster today. Where is the rest of your lot?'

He frowned. 'The rest of...my lot? Safely in their quarters, I would hope.'

'Oh, so you're not playing around here then?'

'No...' he replied with deliberate slowness as if talking to an imbecile.

I straightened and crossed my arms. 'Look, you don't have to keep up this facade with me. You live in the twentieth century and it would be easier for both of us if you stopped the pretence and gave me straight answers.'

My visitor glanced at me and ran his hand through his hair. He shook his head, looking around the room with genuine confusion in his eyes.

'Mistress, I crave your pardon. The...twentieth century?'

When I worked in ER, I encountered people from all walks of life--the drug addicted, the delusional, the paranoid...but this man seemed different. His clear gray-green eyes betrayed puzzlement, but not fear.

'Perhaps if you start by telling me your name?' I ventured.

His fingers drummed on the tabletop. 'Nathaniel Preston of Heatherhill Hall.'

'Heatherhill Hall?'

His eyes brightened. 'Aye. That is my home. You know of it?'

'I've visited it a couple of times. It's only a few miles from here.'

He frowned. 'I am sure I would recall your visit.' For the first time a smile caught at the corner of his lips. 'Particularly if you habitually wear such fetching outfits.'

I ignored the last comment. 'Do you live in one of the cottages on the estate?'

'Of course not. I live in the Hall. My family has owned the manor of Heatherhill for centuries.'

'They may well have done, but, unless you have some sort of caretaker's flat, you can't possibly live there, Mr. Preston. It's been in the hands of the National Trust for years.'

He raised his hand and rubbed his eyes, and his shoulders

slumped. 'Mistress, you truly talk in riddles. Who, or what, is the National Trust?'

I sighed. The pretence had begun to get wearying. He really must have had quite a knock on the head if he actually imagined he belonged in the seventeenth century.

'Are you going to let me look at your head?' I asked.

His hand hit the table and I jumped. 'Mistress, my head is quite clear. I have taken no hit to it. Now if I could trouble you to bind my arm, I will be gone.'

'Your arm needs to be stitched and I do not have any local anesthetic.'

'Do what you must, but hurry. Those scurvy roundheads will no doubt return in search of me, and I have no wish to get you into trouble.'

Scurvy roundheads indeed. I rose to my feet and squinted at the wound. 'Do you want me to suture this now?'

'I do not require you to do anything, mistress.' He sounded exasperated. 'Stitch it or not, it is all one to me.'

'I should take you to hospital.'

The chair screeched on the flags as he pushed himself back from the table. 'Hospital? I am not dying. If it is too great a trouble for you, I assure you my grandmother has skill enough to see to it.'

He rose to his feet and turned for the door, and then as if remembering something, he turned back, a lopsided smile on his face. 'Perhaps if I could trouble you for a loan of a horse, I would be grateful. It is a long walk home. You have my word that I will return it anon.'

I set down the wad of gauze I had been holding and confronted him, hands on hips.

'My horse? I don't own a horse. Look, Nathaniel, you've lost a bit of blood, if you like I can give you a ride home.'

'But you said you had no horse?'

'In the car.' I could not help the exasperation that crept into my voice. His continuing delusion had really begun to concern me. 'Nathaniel, look at me. What year do you think this is?'

'The year of our lord 1645.'

'1645?' I stared at him. 'Nathaniel, it is 1995.'

He narrowed his eyes. 'No, you jest.' He sank back onto the kitchen chair, his eyes glassy.

'I do not jest. Now stay there. I'm going to ring my brother. Perhaps he can talk some sense into you.'

'So it is true,' he muttered more to himself than to me.

Keeping a wary eye on my visitor, I reached for the phone and carried it into the living room while I waited for Alan to pick up.

'Hey, Jess.' Alan greeted me cheerfully.

'Alan, are you busy?'

'I'm correcting papers, nothing I can't put off. Is this important?'

'I have a man in my kitchen who thinks he is living in 1645,' I whispered.

'Sounds like a case for the psychs, not me.'

'Please come over, Alan. There is something about him...sorry I can't explain--'

'Is he threatening you?' My brother sounded alert and concerned.

'No, not at all. He's just a little...confused.'

Alan let out a sigh. 'All right, I'll be there in fifteen minutes.'

I washed my hands in the bathroom and returned to the kitchen. Nathaniel Preston slumped over the table, his head resting on his good right arm, an air of defeat and exhaustion in the line of his shoulders. He straightened as I rustled the packages in my medical bag and selected a sterilized packet with needle and thread.

I pulled on surgical gloves and looked across at him as I tore open the packet. 'This will hurt,' I said.

He raised tired, blood shot eyes to meet mine. 'Do what you must, mistress. I've had worse hurts than this.'

'Jessica. My name is Jessica Shepherd.'

'Mistress Shepherd.' He managed a faint smile, his face pale now alarmingly pale beneath the tan. 'Did you say you were a woman doctor?'

'Yes. Although I'm a pediatrician,' I said.

He frowned. 'Pediatrician?'

'I specialize in children's health.' I held up the needle.

He closed his eyes. 'A doctor for children,' he said quietly, more to himself than to me. 'She was correct.'

'Who?' I enquired.

He gave me a disarming smile. 'No one, mistress. Just do what you need to do and then we must talk.'

The muscles in Nathaniel's jaw tightened as I sutured the wound but to his credit he did not flinch. I followed up with tetanus and penicillin injections, which he bore without complaint.

'Well, I will hand it to you, Nathaniel Preston, you're pretty tough.'

He let out a deep breath. 'I've been hurt before.'

'So I see.' My gaze dropped to the jagged scar below his ribs. 'I didn't realize the Civil War Association could be quite that authentic.'

'What is this Civil War Association of which you speak?'

I looked into his puzzled eyes and shrugged. 'It doesn't matter. You can talk about it with Alan.'

He spread his fingers on the table and looked down at them. 'Mistress Shepherd, is what you say true? Is this the year 1995?'

I nodded. '1995.'

He straightened his arm and grimaced. Recognizing the

pinched look around his eyes and mouth, I stood up. 'Nathaniel. That arm must be hurting like hell. I will give you something for the pain.'

I went to the tap in the kitchen and turned it on. Behind me, the chair scraped, and Nathaniel joined me at the basin.

He ran his hand under the flow of water and as I turned the tap off, he shook his head and said with what sounded like wonder in his voice, 'Do that again.'

I complied. He put his hand on the tap, turning it on and off. Before I could stop him, he'd turned the hot water tap on hard. Scalding water shot from the tap and he drew his hand back.

'Incredible,' he marveled, shaking his hand with a grimace. 'Hot water on command. Do you have a servant to heat it for you?' He looked around the room as if he expected a secreted servant to be hiding in the cupboards.

'No,' I replied, instinctively grabbing his hand and holding it under the cold water. 'I am all out of servants. The gas board does it quite adequately. Let me look at that hand.' He held out his hand but apart from being a little red, there didn't appear to be any damage.

I looked up at him. 'Do you really need me to tell you the red dot means hot water?'

'Red dot...hot water...I will remember,' he mumbled.

He took the pain killers and a glass of water I held out for him, weighing the little pills in his hand. 'What do I do with these?'

'Swallow them.'

The mesmerizing gray-green eyes narrowed. 'Is this poison?'

I shook my head. 'I promise it's not poison and it will take the pain away.'

He swallowed the pills, washing them down with the water, making a face at the bitter aftertaste.

He straightened and picked up my right hand. 'Thank you for your care of me, Mistress Shepherd.'

Before I could react, he kissed my hand. The touch of his lips on my skin had been no more than a butterfly touch, but it sent a lightning bolt through me as if it had ignited a touch paper that could not be extinguished. I withdrew it as if I had been scalded.

His eyes met mine, holding my gaze. 'Jessica Shepherd, are you a good doctor?'

'I believe so.'

He took a breath and leaned against the draining board, running a hand over his eyes.

'Forgive me,' he said. 'Just a little dizzy.'

'You're still looking rather pale. I think you should rest for a little before you go home. Would you like a bath?'

He frowned. 'A bath? Why? I had a bath last month.'

I wrinkled my nose. While not entirely unpleasant, a long run in heavy clothes on a hot day left a lingering scent of unwashed male.

'Without wishing to be offensive, Nathaniel, I would prefer if you did have a bath before lying down on my spare bed. Follow me.'

I threw open the door to the bathroom. 'I will run the bath and that is...' I indicated the toilet, groping for a word he might recognize in his confused state, '...the privy.' I demonstrated its flushing properties. 'Now, towels are here and in the bottle is soap for your hair. You can use this dressing gown.'

I pulled out the large, white, fluffy toweling gown left by Mark, and no doubt "borrowed" from one of the many expensive hotels Mark frequented on his holidays.

My guest seemed more interested in the toilet. He kept pressing the flush button. 'Give it a chance to refill,' I said with infinite patience. 'There, your bath is run. I'll leave you to it.'

As I closed the door on him, I added, 'Try not to get the bandage wet.' I had used a waterproof dressing but knowing men, thought it worth pointing out.

He swept me a low bow. 'Mistress Shepherd, I am indebted to you.'

'I will put some supper on while you have a bath.'

It had been a long time since I had cooked anything more than baked beans on toast and I rather enjoyed the challenge of throwing together a simple meal of spaghetti Bolognese.

As I sliced the onion, tears starting in my eyes, Alan knocked at the kitchen window, nearly causing me to slice my finger.

'So where is your mystery man?' he asked as I let him in.

'Having a bath,' I sniveled.

'It's a bit of a risk inviting strange men into your house, Jess. Why didn't you call the police?'

That was a question I couldn't answer. 'I don't feel threatened by him and there's something about his story that... I don't know--promise me you won't laugh--has a ring of truth to it.'

Alan picked up Nathaniel's torn and stained jacket and shirt from the back the kitchen chair.

He let out a low whistle and I looked up blinking through my streaming eyes.

Alan turned to me, holding the shirt in his hand. 'Jess. This stuff is genuine.'

'What do you mean 'genuine'?'

'The cloth, the hand stitching, the lace. It's all authentic seventeenth century.

'Nonsense. If it was genuine it would be antique, hardly the stuff to wear while you go scrambling over someone's wall or playing your silly war games, come to that.'

'Jessie, I'm telling you, I know all the makers of reproduction clothing, and there is no way they would ever get this degree of accuracy just in the choice of fabric. Look at the blackwork embroidery on the shirt...unless it was purloined from some museum...'

He frowned and screwed his nose. 'But even then it couldn't possibly be in such good condition, bloodstains aside.'

'What do you know about blackwork embroidery?' I scoffed, wiping my eyes on the tea towel.

'More than you,' he countered and turned his attention to the sword, drawing it from its scabbard. He turned the blade over, weighing it in his hand. 'Lovely.'

'A Wilkinson sword?' I grinned at the avaricious glint in his eye.

'Hardly. Jess, this is a genuine seventeenth century sword.' His eyes widened, and he gave a low whistle. 'And if I'm not mistaken, that is genuine seventeenth century blood.'

I glanced at the darkening substance on the sword and recoiled. 'Oh my God, he's killed someone. I'm harboring a mad serial killer.'

'Or he is exactly who he says he is,' Alan responded, his expression grave. 'What does he call himself?'

I reached for a tissue to wipe my nose and said, 'You'll laugh. He says he is Nathaniel Preston of Heatherhill Hall.'

'There was a Colonel Nathaniel Preston living at Heatherhill Hall at the time of the Civil War,' Alan said.

'Are you telling me there is a chance my friend in the bathroom is who he says he is?' I could hardly keep the sarcasm out of my tone.

Alan shrugged. 'There are more things in heaven and earth, Horatio,' he quoted.

'Oh, come on, Alan. You're telling me that while I'm minding my own business in my back garden in June, 1995, a man from the seventeenth century comes over my garden wall?'

'I'm not saying it's logical. I'm just saying strange things can happen.'

I thrust the onions into the pan where they crackled in the hot oil. 'Look, Alan, he's one of your re-enactors who has got himself spaced out on something chemical and thinks he is genuinely from 1645. You were right first time, he probably needs a psych assessment but hey, that's just my professional opinion. Feel free to ignore me.'

'So who is he then?' Alan countered.

'As I told Mistress Shepherd, my name is Nathaniel Preston.' The voice came from the door.

We both started and turned to the doorway, where Nathaniel Preston stood clad only in Mark's purloined dressing gown. I wondered how much of the conversation he had heard.

From the worried look on his face, most of it.

'I assure you both, I am not a...' he looked straight at me, '...mad killer, Mistress Shepherd, or whatever it was you called me. When I awoke this morning it was the third day of June in the year of our lord, 1645. After I broke my fast I set off for Oxford to meet with the king's advisors. It was my misfortune to come upon a forward patrol of Fairfax's men. It is only by God's grace that I made good my escape, but not before I had scored several hits.' He indicated the sword. 'The hurt to my arm was a pistol ball. You may choose to believe me or not. I do not wish to bother you further but I need my clothes.' He pointed at his shirt, still clutched in Alan's hand. 'Then I will be gone.'

'Where to?' I blurted out, breaking the uncomfortable silence.

'Home,' he said, but his voice had lost its certainty.

'Your clothes need cleaning and mending, Nathaniel. I have some other clothes here.' I indicated a neat pile of clothing on the chair, more forgotten items from Mark's time that I'd dredged from the back of the wardrobe where I'd thrown them. 'They may be a little big for you but they'll do for now.'

He picked up the t-shirt from the top of the pile, and turned it around frowning. 'Mistress, I'm no fool but I would appreciate it if you could explain what this is and how I wear it?'

I looked at Alan but Alan wore a button-through shirt. 'Just pull it over your head, and the tracksuit pants...' I mimed, '...you just pull on.'

'And these?' Nathaniel held up the jockey shorts.

I turned to the pan on the stove to hide my laughter. If this was no more than playacting, he was very good.

Mercifully, Alan took charge. 'Mr. Preston, Nathaniel. I'm Jessie's brother, Alan. How about you come with me and we will work this out.'

I heard the wariness in his voice as he said, 'Mistress Shepherd said you are with

Mortlock's Regiment? Can I trust you?'

Alan cleared his throat. 'In the circumstances, Colonel Preston, you can consider me a friend.'

I whirled around, wooden spoon in hand.

Nathaniel straightened. 'You called me Colonel Preston.'

'That is your title, isn't it?'

Nathaniel glanced at me. 'Yes, but I've not mentioned it.'

'Like I said.' Alan put a hand on the man's uninjured shoulder. 'Consider me a friend.'

---

I HAD NEVER THOUGHT it possible for a man to look uncomfortable in tracksuit pants and a t-shirt, but Nathaniel Preston did. He moved as if the very feel of the clothing was alien to him, the way I had seen Alan's re-enactors moving in the unfamiliar boots and heavy clothing of the seventeenth century.

'How's the arm?' I inquired.

He shrugged. 'It will mend. I don't know what was in those objects you made me swallow but I can scarce feel a thing. Thank you for the bath, Mistress Shepherd. If you wish me to empty the tub, I will fetch the bucket.'

'That's fine. I'll do it myself.' I did not feel inclined to explain that he only needed to pull the plug. 'Are you hungry?'

Nathaniel's face brightened. 'I could eat an ox.'

'Good. Well, pull up a seat and I'll serve. Alan, you're staying.' I made it a statement not a question.

Without argument, Alan sat down and I served the spaghetti. Nathaniel stared at the plate and then looked up at me, one eyebrow raised.

'Spa-ghet-ti.' I found myself speaking slowly, as if to a small child.

Nathaniel shot me a glance and watching Alan like a hawk, picked up the fork. This piece of equipment itself seemed to cause him some consternation.

'I have heard tell of these contrivances,' he commented, turning it over in his hand.

'They didn't come into general usage until the Restoration,' Alan said.

'The Restoration?'

'Of Charles the Second.'

Nathaniel laid down the fork and stared at Alan. 'Master Shepherd, your sister tells me the year is 1995.'

'That's right,' Alan agreed.

'As I told her, the year—my year—is 1645.' He ran his hand over his eyes. 'This is surely a nightmare from which I will wake.'

Alan leaned his elbows on the table, pressing his fingers together, the way he would address a tutorial group on an important point. 'Nathaniel, this is no nightmare. Jess and I are quite real,' he paused and glanced at me, 'and, it would seem, we have to accept that you are Colonel Nathaniel Preston of Heatherhill Hall.'

For the first time Nathaniel smiled, a wide, genuine smile. 'You believe me?'

Alan regarded him for a moment. 'I'm not sure. I'm a professor of history, Colonel, and my specialty is seventeenth century, more specifically the English Civil War in Northamptonshire. I know--' He broke off, his face grave. 'I know all about you.'

He caught my eye and I read his thoughts. If this man was Colonel Nathaniel Preston of Heatherhill Hall, then Alan did know all about him. More than this man should wish to know.

Alan cleared his throat. 'Now, either we are all in the middle of the same delusion or the impossible has happened, and somehow time has defied all the laws of physics. Unlike my sister, who is a scientist and therefore naturally sceptical, I am quite prepared to believe you are exactly who you say. So, shall we proceed on the basis that when you awoke this morning it was the third of June 1645, and this evening it is the third of June 1995?'

Three feet of table and three and hundred and fifty years divided the two men as they stared at each other. Nathaniel moved his gaze to me.

'And you Mistress. Do you agree?'

I shrugged. 'I don't know what to believe, Nathaniel.'

'You still think me mad?'

I shook my head. 'No, not mad...delusional perhaps.'

'How can I prove that I speak the truth?' he asked.

I shrugged. 'I don't know. Alan is the expert on seventeenth century history but I'm sure whatever question he could ask you, can be just as easily discovered from a book.'

Nathaniel picked up the fork and studied it intently for a moment. 'You say my home still stands?'

'It does,' Alan said.

'Can you take me there? Will this National Trust person let us in?

I stifled a laugh. 'As long as we pay the right money,' I said. 'We can go in the morning.'

I shot my brother a glance and he nodded agreement.

'Tomorrow then,' Nathaniel agreed.

He plunged the fork into the food, awkwardly twisting the spaghetti in emulation of Alan. He chewed thoughtfully for a moment before declaring, 'This spag-etti is truly excellent. Where does it come from?'

'It originated in Italy,' I said.

'Ah yes, I've been to Italy and I recall eating something similar in Naples. My uncle was not fond of what he called foreign food but I- -' He looked around the table and smiled. 'I like to learn new things.'

---

THE PAIN KILLER, a couple of glasses of wine and the effect of what appeared to be a trying day, told on my visitor and after eating, he excused himself. I showed him to the spare bedroom. He collapsed fully clothed into the bed and appeared to be asleep before I closed the door.

Like a pair of spies from MI5, Alan and I went through his clothing but found nothing that gave any indication of his identity, either in this century or the seventeenth. The only hint was the finely wrought initials NP in the guard of his sword.

'NP, Nathaniel Preston,' Alan said with a shrug.

I gave my brother a narrow eyed glance. 'So, he has a sword with initials that match the name he gave us. That doesn't prove anything.' I traced the intricate fretwork on the hilt of the sword with my finger. 'What do you know about the seventeenth century Nathaniel Preston?'

'He's dead,' Alan replied with a wry smile. I pulled a face at him and Alan shrugged. 'At the start of the war he formed his own local regiment and declared for the king. He fought at Edgehill but spent most of the rest of the war in local defense of this area. A few days before Naseby, he was instrumental in deflecting the parliamentary advance at the battle of Chesham Bridge.'

'When was the battle of Naseby?' I asked.

'The fourteenth of June 1645, just two days after Chesham Bridge.'

'That's in a couple of weeks.'

All humour drained from Alan's face. 'I am not sure going to Heatherhill Hall is such a great idea.'

'Why?'

'Because he may not like what he finds out.' Alan looked into the depths of his coffee mug.

'Like what? That he's dead? I think even he may have worked that out.'

Alan looked up at me. 'That he died at the battle of Chesham Bridge.'

'Oh.' A cold shiver ran down my spine. What it would be like to know the exact date of your death?

I busied myself loading the dirty dishes into the dishwasher. The domestic action gave me time to think. The date of the battle of Chesham Bridge was engraved in the stone of the very bridge itself —Twelfth of June, 1645. Its anniversary would be in nine days time and Alan's re-enactors would be out in force.

'I can't believe you give his story any credence,' I said, slamming the dishwasher shut.

'Sorry, Jess, you may think me mad but I am absolutely convinced he is who he says,' Alan said.

I turned and, seeing the deadly serious look on his face, laughed and rolled my eyes. 'Alan!'

'You don't understand, Jessie. Listen to me and just keep an open mind. If the improbable has happened, and there is some slip in time that has sent Nathaniel Preston from 1645 to 1995, we are going to have to be careful to make sure we don't change history.'

'What do you mean?'

'Imagine if he goes back to his time, knowing all about the Battle of Naseby and convinces the king not to take the field.' He shook his head. 'The whole course of the English Civil War could change. Just think what would have happened if the king had not lost Naseby?'

'Umm...he would have just gone on to lose some other battle?' I suggested.

'Maybe, but maybe not. What if Charles wins the English Civil War all because we meddled with history? There will be no commonwealth and we could still be ruled by a monarch who believes in the divine right of kings.'

'Now, you're being ridiculous,' I said. 'I just think we have someone in the grip of some sort of delusion.' I paused. 'A very convincing delusion... I'm going to bed. You can bunk down in here.'

Alan nodded and I left him sitting at the table no doubt ruminating on how the course of history could be changed. As far as I was concerned, we were in the realms of speculative fiction, but I lay awake for a long time staring at the beams of my precious old cottage and thinking about the man who slept in the room next to mine.

## ❧ 2 ❧

## CONFRONTING THE PAST

*MY NAME IS NATHANIEL PRESTON. I am the owner of Heatherhill Hall and the commander of a company of infantry, mostly my own tenants, for His Majesty, King Charles.*

*My name is Nathaniel Preston...*

*If I say it to myself often enough then it must be true.*

*My arm throbs, a reminder of my own mortality and the fact I am not dead and this is not some strange room in heaven in which I now find myself.*

*I lie in the unfamiliar bed with my eyes closed. I dare not open them for fear the situation in which I have found myself is real.*

*Fool, I know it is real. Is this not what we planned?*

*I can hear their voices downstairs. The man, Alan, who I think, believes my tale and the witch, Jessica, who calls herself a doctor. Whatever potion she gave me ensured I slept through the night but now I sense it is daylight and I must arise and confront this strange new world in which I find myself.*

*I am here because of powerful witchcraft, and what is more, I know the witch. She and I planned this but I never thought...never dreamed...*

*Alice. I call her name in my mind. Now what do I do?*

*For answer, she laughs. She will talk to me when she thinks I am ready to hear.*

———

ALAN SLIPPED out early in the morning and returned before breakfast with jeans, a sweater and shoes for my guest. I poured us both a coffee and we sat talking until Nathaniel emerged, looking like any ordinary male—unshaven, groggy and disheveled with his auburn hair sticking up and Mark's dressing gown loosely belted around his hips. My heart skipped a beat. Even in his tousled state, he looked better than any man I had ever had in my kitchen before.

'How's the arm?' Alan inquired.

'Passing well.' He cleared his throat, sat down at the table and looked at me expectantly.

'Are you hungry?' I asked.

He smiled, the corners of his mouth turning up in a particularly fetching way. 'Ravenous.'

Explaining cereal or toast was beyond me so I did something I have done for no man in my life. I cooked my guest a substantial breakfast of bacon and eggs, a largesse on my part, which Alan indulged in as well.

Coffee was apparently a novelty and not one Nathaniel found palatable until I put two teaspoons of sugar in the cup.

Alan's clothes fitted well but when Nathaniel rubbed at the stubble on his chin, the question of shaving arose. Alan suggested the razor I used for my legs. I glared at him.

'The unshaven look is fine,' I said. 'We can pick up a razor later. Now, what about your hair?'

'What's wrong with my hair?' Nathaniel asked.

The thick dark auburn hair fell to his shoulder. It was the

sort of color many a woman in a hairdresser's would point to with longing. I had a sudden mad urge to run my fingers through it.

'It's fine, but let's tie it back, shall we?' I suggested.

I found a rubber band and tied Nathaniel's hair back in a neat pony tail, allowing me to subtly indulge my desire.

'Very trendy,' Alan remarked.

Very attractive, I thought. With his hair away from his face, I could see the well chiseled cheek bones and strong jaw line. Nathaniel Preston could have graced the cover of any up-market men's magazine.

I allowed my gaze to stray across the expanse of his chest, the well defined lines of his musculature straining beneath the plain t-shirt. While talking with Alan the previous night, I had picked up the sword and been surprised by the weight. Who needed expensive gym memberships when you could spend your day riding horses and wielding weighty weapons?

As I backed the car out of the garage I saw Nathaniel reflected in the rearview mirror. He jumped to one side, his hand going to his left hip, where his sword would have hung, had he been wearing it.

When I stopped the car, he approached it as if it were a wild animal, circling it several times, his hand lightly touching the paintwork.

'Extraordinary. A coach with no horse.' He leaned in through the window. 'How do you make it move?'

I held up the key. 'You turn it on.'

Alan, apparently eager to prove his manhood, lifted the bonnet and the two men inspected the engine. I had never suspected my geeky historian brother had such an intimate knowledge of the workings of cars but, despite his best efforts, even he couldn't supply the answers to all the questions Nathaniel bombarded him with.

'Time to get going. You take the front seat,' I said to Nathaniel.

He folded himself into the front passenger seat and I showed him how to fasten the seat belt.

'Fascinating,' he said, running his hand across the dashboard. 'I have read the writings of Leonardo Da Vinci and he talked of there one day being machines that could propel themselves. He even talked of flying machines. Are there such things?'

'Yes. There are flying machines,' I said in a tone heavy with infinite patience.

As I started the ignition, Nathaniel tensed, bracing his hands against the dashboard as the machine came into life beneath him.

As I turned out of the drive into the lane, he yelled, 'Stop!'

I slammed on the brakes, my heart beating wildly beneath my ribs as I wondered what I had hit.

'What?'

Nathaniel pointed to old Mrs. Blackett pottering into the village on her bicycle.

'That is one of Da Vinci's machines,' he exclaimed

I ignored the chortle from Alan in the back seat and looked at my passenger.

'Listen, Nathaniel, you're going to see many strange things in the short drive to Heatherhill Hall. I'm not going to stop for every single one of them.'

He looked at me and that smile curled the corners of his lips. Damn the man. He may have been three hundred years old, but when he smiled I could forgive him anything.

'I promise to behave, Mistress Shepherd.'

'It's just dangerous, having people yelling in my ear while I'm trying to drive,' I muttered.

Once we hit the open road and I accelerated to forty miles per hour, he flattened himself against the front seat.

'This is very fast,' he murmured.

From the back seat, Alan said, 'You know, Nathaniel, the motor in this vehicle is equivalent to ninety-four horses.'

'Ninety-four horses,' Nathaniel repeated.

I shot him a sideways glance. Men were men of whatever age and, although the knuckles of his hand clutching the seat belt were white, his eyes glittered at the speed and power of my Fiat Punto.

---

HEATHERHILL HALL STOOD, as it had for over six hundred years, nestled in a sprawl of ancient gardens, orchards and woodland, unspoiled by the threat of urbanization creeping from the town which now crowded the park walls.

I turned the car in through the fine eighteenth-century gates and past a neat gatehouse.

'That was not there...' Nathaniel murmured more to himself than to me. He turned to look at me. 'You said yesterday the house is now owned by the National Trust. What or who is that?'

'After the war, these sorts of homes became too hard for private families to maintain,' Alan said from the back seat. 'Your descendant, I suppose, sold it to the nation. It has a fine Inigo Jones dining chamber and Grinling Gibbons carvings on the hall staircase.'

Nathaniel frowned. 'What war...' he began but stopped. 'No, that can wait. My father commissioned Jones. I remember him well, but who is this Gibbons person?'

'After your time,' Alan said.

There were hardly any cars in the visitors' car park. I stopped the car and as Nathaniel unfolded himself from the front seat, he looked around.

'It's quite different. The dog kennels were here and over yonder--the barn has gone.'

I frowned and said, 'Good try, but it proves nothing. I'm sure you could find those details in any history of the place.'

The gravel crunched beneath our feet as we walked up the path toward the house. An elderly woman in a pink cardigan opened the door to our knock.

'My, you are early.' She pointedly checked her tiny wrist watch and looked us up and down. She gave Nathaniel a curious look. 'Come in. That will be three pounds. Do you want a guidebook?'

'Three pounds...but...' Nathaniel expostulated, only to be silenced by a dig in the ribs from Alan.

The woman handed us the explanatory self-guided tour leaflets. Nathaniel took the paper and turned it over several times. He squinted at the floor plan of the house.

'Where is the west wing?' he asked.

The woman looked surprised. 'The west wing? Oh, that was lost in a fire in the mid-eighteenth century and never rebuilt. You must have a good knowledge of the house to know that, young man.'

Nat glanced at me and opened his mouth but I took his arm and led him away before he could say anything

'Okay, I will pay you the west wing,' I murmured. 'Shall we start?'

The tour took us into the large room described on the plan as 'The Great Hall'. Nathaniel went straight to a portrait of a man dressed in the extravagant clothes of the mid-seventeenth century. Long auburn hair tumbled over a wide lace collar that topped a green velvet suit. Every bit the seventeenth-century cavalier, he stood behind a seated woman, his hand resting lightly on her shoulder.

My heart jolted. I had been in this room many times before

but never paid much heed to the portraits. Now two thoughts raced together. Even allowing for artistic license, the resemblance between the man and the portrait could not be denied. If he was not the seventeenth-century Nathaniel Preston then he must be a close descendant.

My second thought came from a distinctly female reaction to the inscription below the painting Nl Preston, Esq. and wife, school of Van Dyck.

And wife...? He was married?

As Alan read the inscription aloud, Nathaniel frowned.

'School of Van Dyck? It was the artist himself. I paid a fortune for that piece of vanity.'

'When was it painted?' I asked.

'The spring of '42. Just before the war. My wife and I had spent the winter with the court and I had it painted for her birthday.'

'Your wife?' I enquired, an unexpected feeling of disappointment lodging in the pit of my stomach.

He nodded, looking at the portrait with his head on one side as if seeing it for the first time. 'Anne.'

'She's probably wondering where you are,' Alan remarked.

He shook his head. 'She was taken from me in childbirth just over two years past.'

'Oh, I'm sorry.' Even as I spoke, it struck me absurd to be commiserating over a recent bereavement that had happened three hundred and fifty years ago. I cleared my throat. 'And the child?'

He straightened. 'Two sons, Christian and Nathaniel.'

'Twins?'

He nodded and his expression softened. 'They are my delight.'

I thought about poor, dead Anne. No wonder the poor

woman had died. The mortality rate for first time mothers at that time was horrendous, particularly in multiple births.

'Stay still,' I commanded and wrenched the rubber band from Nathaniel's hair.

The rough cut auburn hair tumbled around his face just as the woman in the pink cardigan bustled into the room holding a feather duster.

She stopped and gaped at Nathaniel.

'My word. Forgive me saying this, young man, but there is quite a striking likeness. That portrait is of Nathaniel Preston. He was killed during the Civil War.'

Her words were met with a blank silence from Nathaniel. I cast a sideways glance at Alan as the woman prattled on, 'Oh yes. Now let me think. His memorial is in the chapel. You could see for yourself. His son's portrait is there.'

She pointed at the far wall and we all turned to look at a fine portrait of a restoration nobleman. He wore a full-bottomed wig and a pleased expression. On close inspection the inscription read Nathaniel Preston c. 1675.

Nathaniel's expression betrayed no emotion as he studied the portrait of his son. The woman prattled on, apparently oblivious to the tension between the three of us.

'You see that?' She pointed to a glass case near the portrait, containing a blackened sword together with some rusting armor and a moth-eaten leather coat. 'That was Colonel Preston's sword and armor.'

'Can I see it out of the case?' Alan asked. 'I am a professor of history at the university,' he added for good measure.

'Oh no, dear. I couldn't possibly open the case. The conservator would eat me for dinner. You will need to write to him. Enjoy the rest of your visit.' She smiled and flicked her feather duster in the vague direction of the woodwork, leaving us alone in the cold hall.

I looked around at the portraits and weaponry and frayed moth-eaten banners and shivered.

Alan had his nose pressed against the glass of the display case. 'It looks like the same weapon,' he said. 'Nathaniel? What do you think?'

Nathaniel dragged himself away from his portrait and turned his attention to the glass case. 'That's my helmet and breast plate and, yes, that is my sword.'

'Are you sure?'

'It has a nick in the blade about three inches from the hilt and my initials are woven into the basket. I had it made in Germany and it cost me a small fortune.'

'Between the portrait and the sword, you must have had a small fortune to begin with,' I remarked.

He looked at me and smiled. 'My grandfather was one of Elizabeth's merchant seamen. We profited well from his encounters with the Spanish.' He looked up at the beams of the Great Hall. 'So very familiar and yet so different.' He took a breath and gave us both a rueful smile. 'I've seen enough for the moment.'

'Let's get some fresh air,' I said.

Outside on the neatly manicured lawn, Nathaniel sank to the ground and lowered his head onto his bent knees. We sat beside him, grateful for the warm sun after the cold hall.

'Are you sure that is the same sword?' I said at last.

'Without a doubt,' Alan said. He frowned. 'Hang on. You must go back at some point or else how can you be...'

'Killed?' Nathaniel supplied the missing word. He rose to his feet in one swift movement and looked at Alan.

'If you are indeed a student of my times, you will be able to tell me how...how...' He swallowed and without looking at either of us he said in a low voice, 'Perhaps I should see where I lie.'

'Are you sure?' Alan asked. Nathaniel nodded.

On the path through the woods to the little chapel, indicated on the ground plan, we passed an elderly gentleman in a tweed sports coat coming from the direction of the chapel. He inclined his head and wished us all a good morning.

The sign by the door announced that Holy Communion would be held at 9 AM. I glanced at my watch. It was now ten. Alan slowly pushed open the ancient oak door, but the service must have concluded. The building basked in silence. We slipped inside and stood at the door, allowing our eyes to adjust to the gloom. The walls and floors were covered in memorials. Fresh flowers graced the altar, neat stacks of prayer and hymn books and a notice board scattered with notes about the church embroidery group and the fellowship evening were evidence the building was still used.

'Can I help you?' A middle-aged man in a clerical collar came in from the vestry.

'Yes, I hope you can,' Alan said. 'We're looking for the tomb of Nathaniel Preston.'

'Which particular Nathaniel Preston? There are several of them. One in each generation of Prestons, I believe.'

'The one killed in the Civil War.'

'Oh yes, his memorial is over by the chancel.' The priest led the way, chatting to us as he went. 'The writing is fairly worn but I think you can still make it out. Oh dear, someone has put a chair over it. Let me move it.' He pushed the offending chair to one side. 'There you are.'

The three of us stared at the memorial stone set low on the wall. The vicar was right, the inscription was worn and the seventeenth-century script difficult to read. Alan knelt and traced the letters with his fingers.

'In memoriam Colonel Nathaniel Preston of Heatherhill. Born fourteenth November in the year of our Lord 1615. Died at the battle of Chesham Bridge, twelfth June in the year of our Lord 1645.'

'The story is that his body was never recovered,' the vicar said. 'That's why it is only a memorial stone and not a tomb. Well, if you'll excuse me, I must tidy up and be on my way. I only do one service a month here. You were lucky to catch me.'

We thanked him and stood in a semi circle looking down at the memorial stone.

'So you really are a Colonel?' I struggled to keep lightness in my tone.

'Of course. It was my regiment,' Nathaniel snapped. 'What else would I be?'

He turned sharply on his heel and marched out of the chapel, sending daylight streaming into the gloomy building as he opened the door.

'You're the one with the PhD in the subject,' I said to my brother. 'What do you know about him?'

'Preston's Regiment of Foot,' Alan said. 'A minor regiment, but it played a considerable part in the battle of Chesham Bridge, a precursor to Naseby.'

The village of Naseby lay just five miles distant and every year Alan's re-enacting group would participate in some form of muster to commemorate the battle. I had attended a few, and like any local, had become quite familiar with the stories of the battle that had been the last great set piece battle of the Civil War and marked the end of the King's cause.

We found Nathaniel leaning against the car, arms and feet crossed, staring at the gray stone house that had once been his home. He said nothing as I unlocked the car.

'I think we could all do with a drink,' Alan said as I turned the vehicle onto the road.

I glanced at Nathaniel. He stared straight ahead, his face white and drawn. 'I second that,' I agreed.

We found The Bear open, the wooden tables outside already populated with the early lunchtime crowd. We settled ourselves in a secluded corner of the bar and Alan went to fetch three beers.

'I used to come here,' Nathaniel said at last. A wry smile twisted the corner of his mouth. 'It has changed little.'

'Fourteenth-century and proud of it,' I said.

Alan set the beers down and opened a packet of crisps. As one, we lifted the glasses and took long draughts.

'So--' Alan spoke first. 'Nathaniel Preston of Heatherhill Hall, I believe you.'

Every logical instinct in me cried out in resistance. This defied the laws of physics of nature but with a small, shaking voice I said, 'So do I.' Nathaniel looked from one to the other of us. 'And I, you.'

Alan frowned. 'What I want to know is how you come to be here?' Nathaniel picked up his beer and took a swig

'What happened yesterday?' Alan asked. 'Anything...peculiar?'

Nathaniel looked at the table and shook his head. 'Nothing of significance. I told you I had set off for Oxford in the morning, when I encountered the enemy.' He touched his injured arm. 'As Master Shakespeare would say, I decided discretion was the better part of valor and--' That fetching smile caught at his lips again. 'Withdrew.'

'You mean, you ran away?' I said.

He fixed me with an amused smile. 'They shot my horse from under me. I got a little way before it went down and then I was on foot. I was making my way home along the lane that runs beside your cottage with six of the scurvy knaves in hot pursuit and,' he shrugged, 'decided to take cover behind your wall.'

'Did you feel anything? See anything unusual?' Alan leaned forward.

'Yes. I went over a wall and came across a half naked woman,'

Nathaniel said, revealing a sense of humor that transcended the centuries.

'I was not naked,' I protested.

'To my eyes you were, but I now see you were quite properly dressed.' He looked around the bar at the other drinkers. 'My mother would be appalled to see such immodesty.'

'Well, I'm grateful to have been born in the twentieth century.' I raised my glass. 'Here's to the twentieth-century woman.'

Nathaniel smiled and lifted his glass. 'A truly wonderful creation.'

He turned to Alan. 'To answer your question. No, I simply went over the wall.' But even as he spoke, he looked sideways, not quite meeting Alan's eyes. I wondered if, perhaps, there was more to the story than he was prepared to tell us.

'This is extraordinary. A genuine seventeenth-century resource. Imagine what we could do...' Alan sat back, and I recognized the look of excitement on his face. Alan was formulating a plan.

'Alan.' I thumped him on the arm. 'Whatever you are thinking, the answer is no. You're not turning Nat into a side show, and who would believe you anyway?'

Alan stared at me. 'Of course, you're right. Nat--do you mind if I call you that? Nathaniel is such a mouthful--I am a professor at the university. My subject is seventeenth-century history, particularly the English Civil War.'

'What war?' Nat looked at him.

'Your war. We call it the English Civil War, and yes, indeed, it is the subject of much academic interest, just as you probably read about the Wars of the Roses.'

Nat frowned. 'So you can tell me what became of the struggle?'

'I can, but are you sure you want to hear it?'

'Perhaps not right now,' Nat conceded. He set down his beer

and said with a wry, humorless smile, 'It has been enough for me to know that I am dead, and indeed to know the exact date and circumstances of my death.'

I cleared my throat. I had been in the position of passing bad news to patients but even I couldn't tell them exactly how, and when, they would die. Unless one was a prisoner on death row, how does anyone know when they will die? I don't think I would want to have that information and could only imagine what thoughts were going through Nat Preston's mind.

It was the fourth of June. If his time and ours ran parallel, he had eight days to live. Nathaniel tapped his fingers on the table and looked up at Alan. 'So you think that I will return?'

Alan frowned. 'Unless there is another Nathaniel Preston in a parallel universe, then you must go back.'

I shook my head in disbelief and stood up. All my life I had followed only logic and scientific proof. When I tried to make sense of what I was hearing, the thoughts whirled and jostled in my head.

'I can't get my mind around this. Time for another beer.'

I fetched us all another round and when I set the glasses on the table, Alan leaned forward. 'We are agreed that yesterday was the same day of the month, only the year is different?' Nat nodded and Alan continued, 'So it seems to me, unless the fabric of time is going to be completely disrupted, you have to return.'

'What do you mean?' I asked.

Alan cleared his throat. 'We know Nat was present at the Battle of Chesham and his sword is in that display case. Therefore he must return.'

Nat's mouth tightened and the unspoken words lay on the table between us; he had to return to die.

'But how is he going to return?' I asked.

Alan turned to me. 'Jess, what did you feel yesterday?'

'Feel? Nothing. Nat came over my wall and trampled my

dahlias. That's it. There wasn't any weird shimmering or strange music.'

'No, that's not what I meant, but it is probable for those few seconds you were probably there as well.'

'In the seventeenth century? With a Walkman?' I spluttered on my beer.

Alan shrugged. 'I'm a historian, not a physicist.'

'I'm going back to my death,' Nat said.

Alan cleared his throat. 'You may not have a choice. Just as you didn't choose to fall over a wall into the twentieth century, time may take you back when you least expect it.'

Nat drained his glass and set it down with a thump. 'Then life, whatever form it takes, is for the living. I want to know everything about this time.'

---

At the end of a long day, we returned to my little cottage. Alan excused himself to return to his flat in Northampton and his papers, leaving me alone with Colonel Nathaniel Preston.

We had driven around the area, and explored every nook and cranny that he would have known from boyhood--no church or inn or ancient monument in the neighborhood had been neglected. To my surprise, now he had accepted the fact he was in 1995, he seemed to take in every new sight and sound with enthusiasm. In his position, I probably would have crawled under the bedclothes and stayed there, but he had a curiosity that astonished me.

One more modern invention awaited him and I was a bit wary it might lead to sensory overload. The television. When the picture flicked into life, he visibly started but once over the initial shock, crouched in front of the screen, touching the newsreader's image.

'How...' He looked up at me, frowning.

I smiled. He looked so endearing, like a puzzled child, but a day of providing detailed explanations on every facet of twentieth-century life had left me exhausted.

'I have no idea,' I conceded. 'How about I cook us some dinner? If you want to change channels...um, get a different story, then you press this button.' I handed him the remote and, like all males of my acquaintance, he proceeded to channel surf. That kept him busy while I rustled up an omelet and soup for dinner.

I poured us each a glass of red wine and, with a heartfelt sigh, sat on the sofa beside him.

'How is your arm?' I asked, my fingers lightly brushing his injured bicep.

He stretched his arm and flexed his fingers. 'A little sore but bearable.'

'I'll give you another pain killer before bed tonight.'

He smiled. 'They are most efficacious, but I think not. Tell me, Jessica, are there other women doctors in this time?'

'Many of us. Doctors and hospitals are different places today. Yesterday you said you wouldn't go to hospital because you weren't dying.'

'That is the only reason for a hospital.' He shuddered. 'I have read Dr. Harvey's work on the circulation of blood. Is he correct?'

'Yes he was,' I replied.

'I am interested in knowledge.' Nat sipped his wine. 'I like to know why things happen the way they do.'

'Isn't it all the work of God?'

He looked into the glass. 'This is a fine wine.'

'Just an Australian Shiraz,' I said. 'Nothing fancy.'

'What is Australia?'

I found my old school atlas and indicated Australia on the

map of the world. He closed the book and set it to one side, shaking his head.

'I have seen enough for one day,' he said. 'You ask if everything is the work of God? Of course it is but that does not preclude reason. You are a doctor, have you not seen the hand of God where there is no reason?'

'Many times,' I conceded.

'When I was eighteen I travelled on the continent. I spent six months in Italy.'

'Is that where you came across Leonardo Da Vinci?'

'I procured a book of his machines and brought it home with me. It has been my constant companion.' He gave me the benefit of one of his lopsided, wry smiles. 'I even tried to construct one or two of them. Not with any success.'

'You are a contradiction then.' I tilted my head to one side and looked at him. 'From what I know of the seventeenth century, you are a man ahead of your time in many ways.'

'So I have been told,' he commented as he poured himself another glass of wine. 'One of the great scientists of all time, Isaac Newton, was born not far from here in Lincolnshire in 1642. He changed the way we view the world.'

'So there will come a time of enlightenment when this war is done?'

I shrugged. 'I suppose so. Under Charles the Second, Newton and others founded the Royal Society...' His attention had wandered to the flickering TV screen. Perhaps, like me, he had taken in as much as he could for one day. 'Tell me about your family?'

His attention snapped back to me. 'What do you want to know?'

'Your wife?'

'Anne.' He shrugged, a curious dismissive gesture when talking about one's spouse, I thought.

'Had you known her long?'

'It was never intended as a love match, Jessica. Her father was able to provide power and influence at court that my father lacked. He paid a handsome dowry for her hand.' He smiled. My face had always been a book and I must have looked horrified at this cold blooded approach to matrimony.

'You are shocked? I liked her well enough but she didn't understand me...my interests. Her only thoughts were of the house and children.'

'And your children?'

'Just the boys.' His mouth tightened. 'They are my greatest concern. I abhor the world in which we now live, a country at war with itself, and I fear for them. You have no children?'

I shook my head. 'No.'

'And why do you have no husband?'

I couldn't answer that. I would have married Mark, until the 'incident'. I looked up and saw Nathaniel looking at me.

He arched an eyebrow knowingly. 'A broken heart, I think?'

I managed a watery smile. 'Something like that.'

'Then whoever he is, he is entirely undeserving of your grief.' He brushed my cheek with a finger and a shiver ran down my spine. 'You are a lovely woman, Jessica. There will be others.'

'Not many men like playing second fiddle to a career, particularly when they have one of their own. But enough of me. What about your parents?'

'Both dead. My sister still lives at the Hall and my grandmother, Dame Alice.' He looked at me and smiled. 'You would like Alice. She is--' He leaned forward and put his head in his hands. 'I am tired, Jessica. Would you excuse me if I retired for the night?'

As he rose to his feet, I asked, 'Can you work the bath?'

'Another bath?' he inquired with a raised eyebrow. 'I only had one yesterday?'

'Well, these days we bathe daily,' I told him, adopting a severe expression while trying to keep a smile off my lips.

'Too much bathing can sap your strength,' he replied.

'Nonsense. Just call it a house rule. Good night, Nat.'

'Good night, Jessica.' A slow smile spread across his face. 'My witch.'

I felt an unfamiliar warmth wash over me. Mark never had any terms of endearment to describe me. 'Why do you call me that?'

'Because you have bewitched me.' He bowed and left the room.

I heard the bath water running and sat back, nursing my glass and thinking about the curious man who had dropped into my life. My safe, clinical world had been turned upside down and, I thought, even if Colonel Nathaniel Preston were to leave tomorrow, it would never be quite the same again.

---

*I CANNOT SLEEP.*

*Every time I close my eyes I see this new world and all its wonders. The noise overwhelms me. Even now in the dead of night, I hear the carriages racing past and see the bright lights illuminate the curtains over the windows.*

*Light. There is so much light.*

*I try to order things in my understanding, relate them to my own time, but I fail. My own ignorance fails me. I am a savage in this land. Jessica the Witch must think me a veritable fool, and that concerns me. I think of her warm, sun-touched skin on that day I first saw her, and the courage with which she faced me. I want to touch her. I need that touch of a warm, living being to remind me that I am still a man and not an object of pity.*

*The knowledge of my death tugs at my mind. I keep pushing the memory of that cold stone in the chapel away. I don't believe I am to die. I am only thirty years old. I have two small sons. Who will care for them? Who will protect my sister and my grandmother?*

*Alice. Help me. I can't live with this knowledge.*

*I hear her voice coming through the mist of my mind. 'You must find the strength. Remember why you are there. Learn as much as you can of this new world Nathaniel, and you will have a chance to set things in order.'*

*I close my eyes and remember all we talked about, Alice and I. She is right, I have to acquire the knowledge needed to set my world in order.*

*But to do that I will return to my time.*

*To do that, I must die.*

# 3

## NORTHAMPTON

So many books.

Jessie the Witch must put great store by learning. Not since the great library at Oxford have I seen such a collection. Every book I own is precious to me and cost dearly. I sometimes closet myself in my library and take each one out for the sheer pleasure of the touch of the paper and the smell of the leather binding.

There is one book more precious than all the others that I keep locked away and only bring out when I want to dream. I have thought much about it in the last few days.

In a glass cabinet, Jessie has an odd assortment of broken pottery and keys. My breath stops in my throat as I recognize one of the objects. Despite the rust, it is still familiar, just as my sword had been. Such a little thing but is this what binds us?

'Why is this here?' I ask Alice.

'You will know in time,' she replies.

I CAME BACK from my morning run to find Nat fully dressed, standing in front of the cabinet containing the odd pieces of the cottage's past that I had found during the renovation. I have enough interest in history to appreciate the value of the broken bits of pot, old bottles, bits of clay pipe and other pieces of household detritus that kept turning up as I worked on the house. They told the story of the previous inhabitants, and their story had become the story of the house.

I particularly liked the keys, which ranged from a giant iron door key to small cupboard keys and one particularly interesting item with the rusted remains of a fine filigree pattern on its head.

He turned around as I entered, inclined his head and smiled.

'I have been looking at your books.' He waved a hand at my overfilled bookcases. 'You must be wealthy to possess so many books.'

I laughed. 'No, I'm not. It's just that books are cheap and I'm a voracious reader.'

His eyes met mine and he smiled. 'Then you are blessed. Even I can only afford the luxury of purchasing a book every now and then.' He frowned and looked me up and down. 'What is that strange garb you are wearing?'

I sat and unlaced my running shoes. 'I've just been for a run.'

His left eyebrow shot up as it did when some new concept intrigued him. 'Who were you running from?'

'No one. I just went for a run. It's how I keep myself fit.'

'The women of my household have no need of running.' He narrowed his eyes, as if imagining the women of his household out for a morning jog.

'From what I know of housekeeping in your era, I'm sure they didn't need to do any extra exercise. I, on the other hand, have a stressful job and I find going for a run in the morning helps clear my thoughts for the day.'

He shook his head as if the concept utterly defeated him. 'Perhaps I will come for a run with you, just to see what magic there is about it that has eluded me thus far in my life?'

I padded barefoot into the kitchen.

'You're quite welcome but we will need to get you running gear—suitable clothes for running,' I said as I busied myself with making coffee.

He followed me into the kitchen, and leaning against the kitchen bench, looked me up and down, taking in my black singlet and matching leggings.

'They make clothes just for running?' That now familiar smile curled the corner of his mouth 'They suit you.'

I felt a different heat color my cheeks and changed the subject. 'So you like my books? Are you only interested in books on science?'

He considered that question for a moment before replying. 'Science? What is that?'

I cast around for another word. It never occurred to me that the word did not exist in 1645.

'Knowledge.'

'No, I like poetry too. Have you read the works of Dr. Donne?'

I set the kettle down with a thump. 'I love Donne. I even took an extra subject at university to study poetry.'

'So, perhaps we are not so very different?' Nat straightened and came to stand behind me as I plunged the coffee. With his voice lowered, he quoted,

'If thou be'st born to strange sights, Things invisible to see,

Ride ten thousand days and nights, Till age snow white hairs on thee, Thou, when thou return'st, wilt tell me,

All strange wonders that befell thee,...'

No one had ever quoted Donne to me before my first coffee of the day.

He had a rich timbre to his voice and an unusual accent, neither local nor posh

Even without looking at him, his proximity and maleness overcame me and the hairs on the back of my neck stood up. . By the standards of his day, he might have been considered tall but for me was just right. All I had to do was lean back and my head would rest against his shoulder... turn around and put my arms around him... look up at him and place my lips against his. At the last thought, an unfamiliar warmth ran through me as I realized that was exactly what I wanted to do.

The coffee spilled onto the bench.

'Ouch.' Hot coffee slopped on my bare foot and the moment passed.

I cooked bacon and eggs again.

'This is the last time, Colonel Preston,' I said, setting our breakfast plates down; his bacon and eggs and my muesli.

'What is that hen's feed you are eating?' Nat peered into my bowl.

'Muesli. I have to go back to work tomorrow and you will have to fend for yourself.'

He cast a glance at the stove. 'Ah, then you will need to show me how to work your machines.'

At the mention of my 'machines,' a smile caught at the corner of his mouth and I was reminded of a youthful Alan intent on mischief. A sudden vision of the chaos that could meet me on return from work caused me to reconsider.

'We'll talk about it later,' I said. 'I think perhaps we should go shopping in Northampton today.'

'Shopping?'

'If you are going to be staying a while, you need some clothes and other necessities.'

He curled a lock of his hair around a finger. 'I have been observing the men of this age and I think I should cut my hair. I thought at first they must all be poll heads but it seems to be the fashion of this day.'

'Men wear their hair many lengths. You don't need to cut it.'

'But I think I will stand out less if I look much like other men, even if my speech betrays me.'

'I like the way you speak,' I said with a smile.

I jumped at a sharp rap at the door. 'That's probably Alan,' I said, rising to my feet.

I threw open the door Alan's name on my lips.

Mark loomed in the doorway. I stifled a gasp and took a step backward.

'Hello, Jess.' He leaned an arm against the door jamb and smiled at me. 'I thought as we both had the day off, I'd see what you were up to.'

'You could have rung. As it is I have plans, Mark.' I said, conscious that Nat had moved up behind me.

'Oh?' Mark glanced at the man behind me.

He glanced at me expectantly and seemed to be waiting for me to introduce Nat but I couldn't find the words.

'I don't think we've met. Mark Westmacott.' Mark straightened and held out his hand.

Nat looked at the hand and then grasped it firmly. I had the pleasure of seeing Mark wince at the strength of Nat's grip.

'This is an old family friend, Nathaniel Preston. He's just visiting for a few days,' I managed.

'Really?' Mark sounded skeptical. Even though our relationship had ended months ago, at my behest after I caught him in bed--my bed--with one of the interns, he still exerted a proprietary air over me when he could.

'He's asked me to show him around,' I added, conscious of Nat's proximity and a protective hand resting on the small of my back. My skin jumped at his touch.

'Well, I won't bother you then. You clearly don't need any

additional company. I'll see you at work tomorrow,' Mark said with what I recognized as a false cheerfulness. 'Good to meet you, Preston.'

As I closed the door behind my erstwhile lover, Nat regarded me with a quizzical look. 'He seems to think he has some claim on your affections.'

'Oh, was it that obvious? Well, he did for a while but it's over, long over,' I added.

Nat frowned and glanced at the door. 'I'm not sure he feels quite the same way.'

I picked up a cushion and threw it at Nat. He ducked. 'That is none of your business.'

'I'm afraid, Mistress Shepherd, you have become my concern.'

He retrieved the cushion and threw it back at me. I caught it and restored it to the sofa, sitting down with a thump.

'Mark and I were engaged to be married. I found out he had other women so I ended it. He's one of those men who are too used to getting their own way, and he can't seem to understand what he did wrong. It makes it awkward at work.'

Nat sat in the armchair. 'He is a doctor too?'

I nodded. 'A pediatric heart specialist. He is one of the best but there is a certain arrogance that goes with the title of surgeon.'

Nat nodded. 'He is a doctor of the heart?'

'Yes. He specializes in children.'

He smiled. 'I fear your Doctor Westmacott does not truly understand the workings of the heart, to leave yours broken.'

I rose to my feet again and smiled. 'The heart heals, Nat. It's the memories that don't go away. Come on, if we are going to beat the crowds we had better go now.'

We drove into Northampton, an old town that boasted a busy main street with all the shops I needed to outfit my cavalier.

Nat stared at the bustling modern streets. 'I knew this town well.'

'Different?'

'Unrecognizable.'

A group of young girls in tight jeans and brief tops crossed in front of us at the lights. Nat cast a sideways glance at me. 'I don't think I will ever get used to the sight of women in breeches, although I will always treasure the memory of my first sight of you.'

'I'm wearing a skirt today,' I pointed out.

We parked, and I headed straight for Marks and Spencers. Nat strolled beside me, his gaze lingering a little too long on the pretty girls in their summery fashions. One of the more exotic lingerie shops particularly caught his attention. I caught his arm and wrested him away.

'You men are all the same.'

He looked at me with wide, innocent eyes and a half smile indicating he knew exactly what I meant.

'Jessie.' I turned at the sound of my name, my heart falling at the sight of Jenny Young, one of the young doctors from the hospital, pushing her way through the crowd to reach me.

Wasn't anyone at work today?

Mark had been bad enough, but Jenny, sweet girl though she was, could be something of a gossip.

'Hi, Jenny.' I forced a smile and when she looked enquiringly at Nat, added, 'Jenny, this is an old family friend, Nat Preston.'

To my mortification, Nat executed a courtly bow in the middle of High Street. Jenny's eyes widened and she giggled.

'Nice to meet you, Nat.'

'Nat is one of Alan's re-enactor friends. He likes to practice,' I extemporized.

'Oh, I did wonder,' Jenny said. 'Such fun. I've been thinking of joining, particularly,' she added sotto voce to me, 'if they all look like your friend.'

'Trust me, they don't,' I said. 'Jenny works with me at the hospital,' I explained to Nat.

'Are you a doctor?' Nat inquired.

'A very new one,' Jenny replied. 'I've just finished my rotation through pediatrics. Jessie's a terrific role model and fabulous with kids.'

Nat gave me one of those glances I now recognized as betraying a break down in language.

"Well, thank you for that vote of confidence.' I took Nat's arm and gave him an engaging smile. 'If you'll excuse us, we have quite a long shopping list. See you tomorrow, Jenny.'

'Great,' I muttered to myself as we walked away.

'What's the matter?'

'It'll be all over the hospital in the morning.'

'What will be?'

I smiled and thought of Mark. Maybe a bit of gossip wouldn't be a bad thing.

Nat went silent before looking at me with a frown. 'You look after goats?' 'What?'

'Mistress Young said you were fabulous with kids.'

I sighed. 'Children. Kids is another word for children. Ah, Marks and Spencer.'

I had forgotten how tedious shopping with men can be, but fortunately Nat seemed content to let me do the choosing. Good choices too, if I say so myself.

He looked at the shopping bags. 'How long do you think I will be staying?' he asked. 'There are more clothes here than I have owned in my entire life.'

I hated to admit that I had enjoyed shopping for him, even when he jibbed at the endless 'trying on' and left me to guess suitable sizes. It wasn't hard. Nathaniel Preston had the sort of build that would make a garbage bag look like a million dollars.

We managed to find a hairdresser open for business. Nat tugged the rubber band from his hair and regarded it curiously, stretching it experimentally with his fingers as we waited for the girl to finish with her last client.

'Are you sure you want to do this?' I asked.

He nodded. 'I feel like I am standing with a foot in two worlds at the moment. And if you are going to keep making me take baths every day, trust me, a polled head would be a great advantage.'

I was hardly going to suggest the judicious use of a shower cap so I let the barber have her way and the centuries fell to the floor at her feet.

The result took my breath away. If I'd thought him an attractive man before, the transformation of barbered chin and freshly cut hair only served to highlight those stunning gray green eyes. No wonder Jenny had been reduced to a giggling mess.

'It's a little early, but there is a lovely little restaurant by the river we could go to for lunch.' The heat rose to my face, like a schoolgirl asking a boy to go to the movies. 'But it's a little early yet.'

'Ah, the river. I recall it well.' A lazy half smile curled his lips and he looked past my shoulder as if he seeing that time so long past. Bringing his attention back to me, he said, 'Shall we go for a walk along its banks?'

'Are you in the habit of taking strolls along the banks of the Nene?' I asked

'Maybe once or twice, and always in the company of a pretty maid.'

'I think you may find it changed,' I warned.

The River Nene flows through Chesham but downstream where it flows through Northampton it is not a pretty river. Modern buildings crowd the riverbanks and although the canal boats pulled up to the quays relieve the drabness it is not my favorite place to walk. I steered us in the direction of Becket's Park, a patch of greenery among the dull modern buildings.

He took my hand. Strong, calloused fingers tightened on mine and I shivered, thinking of the contrast with Mark's almost delicate surgeon's hands. Mark took better care of his hands than I did.

'And where do you end up?' I laughed as I extricated my hand.

He turned wide, guileless eyes on me. 'Mistress Shepherd, I am a gentleman. May I not be permitted to hold your hand?'

'It depends on your intentions, good sir,' I said with a laugh and held out my right hand as I imagined a seventeenth-century lady of quality would have done.

He took it in his fingers and regarded it for a moment. 'I see you are no gentlewoman. This hand has seen rough work.'

'What it has seen is too much hospital disinfectant.'

He turned it over and raised it to his lips, kissed each finger in turn. My knees weakened and my breathing became ragged.

He looked up at me and I saw the now familiar twinkle in his eye. 'You have never been courted?'

'Not like this,' I conceded. 'Video and a takeaway curry was Mark's idea of romance.'

'Then I am pleased there are some things I can teach you,'

He enclosed my hand in his and we resumed our stroll along the willow-lined path.

'Have you ever been in love?' I asked.

He paused before answering. 'Many times. My first love was the stable hand's daughter.'

'Hardly suitable for the son of the house.'

'Hardly,' he agreed. 'My mother sent her away.'

'Your second love?'

His face softened. 'In Italy. I lived there for nearly a year.'

'What happened?'

He shrugged. 'I knew I had to marry Anne, so at the end of my time I came home, but I think of her often.'

'And Anne?'

The corners of his mouth tightened. 'I've told you. Ours was not a love match. I liked her well enough, and perhaps in time we would have come to love each other, but God took her before her time.'

What a contradiction this man was, I thought--the soldier and scientist with the heart of a poet. If I had met him at a party in an ordinary course of my life, I could quite easily let myself fall for him.

What did I mean?

I had already set myself on that slippery slope. I was strolling along the river bank on a beautiful summer's day with my hand in his. I could forget that he would die in a few short days...that he was already dead and had been for over three hundred years.

I released my hand and stopped.

'Did I say something to offend you?' he inquired.

'No, not at all. I was just thinking...your stay here is transient. I don't want to...'

*Don't want to do what, Jessie? Let yourself fall in love with this man? Too late.*

'I just don't have time for love or romance or any of that nonsense.' I said.

'Master Westmacott has much to answer for.'

I closed my eyes to fight back the tears and sensed, rather than saw him draw near. He folded me into his arms and I found I couldn't resist leaning my head against his chest. He smelled of my soap and something else, spicy and foreign.

His lips brushed my hair. 'Jessie, my witch,' he whispered.

'I'm such a fool.' I sniffed. 'I only met you two days ago and you don't even belong here. You could be whisked away at any moment and then where will that leave me?'

His chest rose and fell beneath my cheek as he sighed and his breath whispered past my cheek as he replied, 'I do not know the answer to that question, Jessie. I'm here for a reason. It was not some momentary lapse in God's concentration that sent me over your wall.'

'A reason? What reason? How--'

He laid a finger against my lips. 'Later.' He stroked the hair back from my face and smiled down at me.

The blood coursed through my veins in a way that would have given Dr. Harvey pause. Whatever had brought him here didn't matter, not for this moment.

He continued. 'You are right, Jessica. I know I must go back to my death. That is my fate and cannot be changed. I would rather die in the knowledge that, for a few brief moments, I had some happiness with a woman who intrigues me beyond measure.' He smiled and tugged gently at a lock of my hair.

'That is the corniest pick up line I have heard,' I muttered as his lips touched mine, stifling my objections.

It may have been corny but it was effective. I would have given myself to him there and then on the bridle path.

I closed my eyes and parted my lips, devouring the taste of him. In my carefully ordered life, the pattern of time had not only been disrupted, but had given me the opportunity to forget for a while that I was a sensible, responsible doctor. For a fleeting moment I could just be a woman; a woman responding to a man in a way she had never experienced before.

I stood poised on the edge of a cliff from which I might never return. He could be gone tomorrow, tonight even, and I would be left forever wondering what it would be like to lie in his arms. We parted and I leaned my head against his chest. He rested his head on mine, engulfing me in his strength and solidity. I closed my eyes listening to the steady rhythm of his heart against my cheek.

I don't know how long we just stood there in the middle of the path, lost in each other. He straightened and looked down the path we had just walked. As we parted, I fought to restore my breathing to normality, and saw what he had seen, a pair of lovers, arms entwined around each other, walking toward us.

'The restaurant is just along here,' I said, my voice quavering with emotion. He looked down at me and smiled. 'Do they serve a good meat or a pie? I fear you are starving me, Mistress Shepherd.'

'They do an excellent steak,' I replied with a smile.

As we turned toward the town, he put his arm around my shoulder. I felt its weight, warm, reassuring and decidedly alive, and slipped my arm around his waist and we strolled like the lovers we passed, toward Northampton.

---

THE COSY NOOK had been a favorite restaurant for Mark and I. Mark would ridicule its kitsch name but he could not deny the food was good. The host, who knew me of course from those trysts with Mark, didn't bat an eye when I arrived without a booking and in the company of a different man.

He seated us outside on the broad terrace overlooking the river where we could watch the colorful canal boats tied up to the riverbank. The delicious warmth of the English summer day folded us in its velvety embrace.

On a whim, I requested two glasses of champagne.

Nat took a tentative sip and pulled a face. 'I would rather have ale.'

I smiled. 'For us, champagne represents good fortune, something to be celebrated.'

'And what are we celebrating?'

'I don't know,' I admitted.

A triumph over the immutable laws of nature and physics? Proof there really are more things in heaven and earth than are dreamed of in our philosophies, or was it simply that whatever the years between us, just for today, just for this moment, we were a man and a woman enjoying a lovely meal in a beautiful place.

I ordered a beer for Nat and finished off his champagne.

'What would you do if you had to make a choice, Nat?' I asked at last.

'A choice between my time and this one?' He sighed and looked away at the canal boats below us. 'There is so much here.' I could hear the hunger in his voice. 'The war is killing my spirit, Jessie. I take no pleasure in fighting my own countrymen and, even worse, having to watch my own people die.'

'Then why are you fighting?'

'Did I have a choice? I have served the king at court. I owe him my complete loyalty.'

'He is going to lose, Nat. The next battle, Naseby, will be his last. After that his cause is lost.'

'So Alan tells me.' Nat's lips compressed in a grim line. 'I won't see it. I will already be dead.'

I looked away, tears springing to my eyes. He reached out and stroked my cheek.

'I can't change history,' he said gently. 'I don't want to change history. Imagine if I go back and tell the king not to take the field at Naseby...what difference will that one conversation make to what is to come?'

This was the same conversation I'd had with Alan.

I shook my head. 'Maybe none.' I sighed. 'What it might do

is prolong the war. I know the king's forces are spent and are no match for parliament's New Model Army. They will have to meet someday.'

He smiled. 'For someone who professes to know nothing of history, you are well informed.'

'You don't have a brother like Alan and not pick something up, but don't tell him.' I smiled in return

He traced a pattern on the back of my hand with his finger. 'To return to your question, Jessie. I am not sure it will be something about which I have to make a decision. My grandmother...' He broke off and picked up his beer, swilling the contents.

'What about your grandmother? You mentioned her before. What has she to do with this?'

He set down the empty glass and sighed. 'My grandmother is the one who has sent me out of time.'

'That's ridiculous. What is she? Some sort of witch?'

'Yes.' The word hung on the air between us.

I gave a nervous laugh. 'Now you're being seventeenth century. Whatever else you may believe, there are no such things as witches.'

He raised an eyebrow. 'No? Then why am I here? Dame Alice knew what she was doing when she sent me to you.'

'But how could she possibly know me? Know about me?' A foolish thought crossed my mind. 'Maybe it is not about me, but the cottage? When I bought the cottage a year ago, it had been empty for decades and before that there had been little done to it. Until I moved in and renovated, it would have looked almost the same to you as it did to the last owner.'

'Now it is you who are being fanciful,' Nat said.

I shook my head. 'No, I think the key to this is the cottage. It is the one link between your time and mine.'

He shrugged. 'It's only a link. I could just have easily walked into the Church of St. Matthew at Chesham. That is little changed.'

'Then tell me about your grandmother?'

'No. We have talked enough about my family. What of your family?'

'Just Alan and I. Our parents were killed in a car accident five years ago.'

I felt the gaping hole in my chest that their deaths had left, as it always did at mention of them. Nat's fingers tightened on mine.

'I am sorry to bring back such painful memories.'

I shook my head. 'It's silly. After all this time I shouldn't get emotional but I do. I miss them every day...' My voice quavered and it was my turn to look away.

Nat stroked my cheek again, curling a lock of my hair around his finger.

'Tell me, Jessie, my witch, has anyone told you recently how lovely you look with the sun on your hair?'

My expression must have given him the answer because he laughed. 'I see another failing in the good Master Westmacott.'

I pushed the vegetables around my plate with my fork. Mark had never told me I looked lovely. He had told me he admired my professional skills or that I had cooked a nice meal, but never had he spoken to me the way this man did.

'Modern courtship is not like that,' I muttered.

He tilted my face up to look at him. 'Then I have something to teach you after all.'

I gave a snort of laughter. 'I know all about seventeenth-century men. There was nothing in their books about pleasing the lady.'

The gray-green eyes closed for a moment before he said, 'Not all men.' He looked at me with a fierce intensity, and my breath caught in my throat. 'You forget I have lived in Italy and some time in France.'

His gaze held mine. Mesmerized, I found myself unable to break eye contact. I wanted to drown in those mysterious depths.

'And what did you learn in Italy and France?' I whispered, hardly trusting myself to speak.

He picked up my hand and turned it over. He lifted the palm to his lips, brushing it with the softest butterfly touch and my breath caught in my throat. His lips moved to my inner wrist. The blood in my veins jumped and my eyes closed. I should have snatched my hand away, sent for the bill, but I couldn't move. It was as if I had melted into the chair.

'I found another book of poetry on your shelves this morning,' he said. 'Andrew Marvell? 'If I had world enough and time, this coyness lady were no crime...' He lowered my hand, caressing the palm with his thumb. 'I don't have world enough and time, Jessica.'

'No,' I whispered hoarsely, 'and no one has ever called me coy. I'll get the bill.'

---

WE SPOKE little on the drive home. We didn't need to. The air between us crackled as if it were charged.

I parked the car in the drive and barely had time to press the lock button before he caught me in his arms. The warm evening closed in on us as his lips met mine. My heart beat so hard, I felt sure he could feel it through my cotton dress.

His fingers meshed my hair, pulling the light combs free. I tugged at his t-shirt, until my fingers glided across the smooth, hard contours of his back. I could scarcely breathe as our lips touched. I closed my eyes, drowning in the moment, wanting it never to end.

'Key,' I mumbled, breaking contact and scrabbling by touch for the lock on the front door.

The door yielded and we stumbled across the threshold. It closed behind us with a thump as Nat booted it shut with his foot. He lifted me as if I weighed no more than a feather and carried me upstairs to my bedroom, where he unceremoniously dumped me on the bed then rapidly divested himself of his disheveled clothing.

I have heard men described as beautiful but as a doctor I had never found the male body particularly attractive. Well, most male bodies. Nathaniel Preston looked pretty good for someone who was nearly four hundred years old. I may have already remarked that his chest and arms would do credit to a determined body builder. The flat planes of his stomach tapered to narrow hips and strong, lean rider's legs.

My breath came in short gasps as he knelt over me.

'I wish you were wearing that fetching outfit I first beheld you in,' he murmured. His eyes appeared to gleam, reflecting the light from the hall. 'I think I like the twentieth century. Now off with that ridiculous chemise.' He tugged at my summer dress. I heard fabric rip but didn't care.

He stopped.

'What is that?' he inquired, and I realized he referred to my bra.

After much deliberation that morning, I had selected a lacy piece of nonsense with matching briefs. A slow smile creased the corners of his eyes. From the way he looked at me, I may as well have been wearing a red satin bustier and crotchless knickers. I didn't know whether to feel incredibly sexy or somewhat guilty.

'My...er...corset?' I ventured.

He laughed and lay beside me, propping himself up on one elbow while he explored the intricacies of the modern brassiere, running his finger around the beribboned edge. The exploratory finger never quite brushed my nipples which ached for him. When I caught his eye I could see he was teasing me.

He slid his fingers around the back and encountered the fastening. His eyelids flickered in concentration, and with one hand, he undid the hooks and eyes with a dexterity that would have done credit to any modern Lothario.

He pushed the inadequate lace confection aside, and his gaze lingered for a moment on my breasts before he bent and kissed first one and then the other, flicking his tongue at my nipples. My back arched. I could have screamed, in my desperation for him.

I don't know what sort of education had been intended for him on his 'grand tour' of the continent. A handsome young man in possession of a good supply of gold coins would have found no shortage of interesting women, willing to impart their knowledge to him. Nat gave me good cause to thank those nameless ladies for their generosity of spirit.

Time stood still. Three hundred and fifty years may have stood between us but I knew I had found my soul mate. We were meant for each other. I closed my eyes and willed myself to forget everything except this man and the touch of his lips and his hands.

Afterward, as we lay tangled in each other's limbs and the bedclothes, I spared a brief thought for Mark, and my other lovers, who had approached lovemaking in much the same way as they took to the cricket field--pads on and straight bat. Nat had none of that twentieth-century reserve.

'What are you thinking?' he asked.

I propped myself on one elbow and ran my fingers through the hair on his chest.

'I was wondering about your wife,' I said.

His lips tightened. 'Anne was not like you. I tried to teach her but she didn't want to know. She was a godly woman who believed intercourse was for one purpose only, the begetting of children.'

I kissed him gently. 'Then that, I am afraid, was Anne's loss. Now it is my turn...' I straddled his hips and took charge.

## ❧ 4 ❧

# THE RULES OF CRICKET

BEYOND THE WINDOW, the birds begin their morning song. Some things never change. At home I would hear the voices of the servants, who awake long before the dawn. Here are only the birds and the occasional passing carriage.

Jessie the Witch lies in my arms, her hair spread across my chest. It is the color of the dark honey Alice would bring in from the hives in the orchard and smells just as sweet, but I know the smell comes from the strange soap in a bottle she keeps in the room with the bath.

'Alice?' I call her in my head. 'Is this what you intended? That I should fall in love with a woman who is not of my time?'

I hear her say, 'Yes, that is how it should be. You are meant to be together.'

'But I am to die. I cannot leave her to mourn me.'

'We all must die,' Alice answers me.

At that thought my flesh turns cold. I kiss Jessie's hair and she murmurs in her sleep and holds me closer. I cannot die, not yet. Not when I have found my soul mate.

I WOKE and found my limbs still tangled in Nat's as if I hadn't moved all night. Stretching my body against his, I sighed in contentment.

'You're awake? Do you mind if I move my arm? I can't feel my fingers,' Nat said rather unromantically.

I rolled off his chest and lay on the pillows, looking up at the ceiling. I smiled and raised a hand to touch my lips, which still tingled from the previous night, as I remembered.

Beside me, Nat lay back and watched me, his hands behind his head. He had the sleek, contented air of a lion that had just eaten its fill. I shivered as I thought of the feline analogy. No lover I had ever been with had given me what I had experienced last night.

I stole a glance at the clock radio beside the bed and sat bolt upright. Nat rolled over and propped himself on an elbow. 'Jessie? Are you all right?'

'It's seven,' I said. 'I'm due at work in half an hour. I'm going to be late.'

He put his hand over mine. 'Don't go.'

It would have been so easy to ring in sick and just lie beside this man, but I swung my legs off the bed.

'I have patients,' I said, bending to kiss him, 'but you know something? I'm going to take some long overdue leave from tomorrow.'

I didn't speak the words hanging over our heads. We didn't know how much time we had so we needed every minute of every day.

'What do you suggest I do today?' he inquired as I scampered around the bedroom retrieving my work clothes.

'Alan said he would call in this morning. I think he's up to something.'

Fully dressed, I bent and kissed him on the lips, resisting the strong hand that wound around my neck, pulling me into bed.

'I'll be home by six tonight,' I promised. 'And then we can plan for the next few days. I have so much to show you.'

The corners of his lips twitched into a smile. 'If they are as interesting as last night, I can hardly wait. Hurry home, Mistress Shepherd.'

***

'WELL, LOOK AT YOU!' my dear friend, Lily French, announced when I arrived late for work, breathless and disheveled. 'The rumors must be true.'

'What rumors?'

'This is a hospital, Jess. There are no secrets. According to the gossip, you were seen yesterday in Northampton with a cute guy.' She smiled. 'And the best bit, Mark is walking around with a face like the grim reaper.'

A satisfied smile tugged at the corners of my mouth and Lily gasped. 'Oh, it's true. Who is he? Go on, tell.'

'At break,' I said. 'I have patients waiting for me.'

When I fetched my coffee later that morning, I had to remind myself to be careful about what I said to Lily, who waited for me at a table in the canteen. Like any woman in love, I longed to share it all, but this story was one too strange for the telling. While falling in love with a man I had only met three days ago might not sound so strange, there was the little matter of an age difference that defied explanation.

'So?' Lily wheedled, raising a cup of canteen tea to her lips.

I shrugged. 'What's to tell? He's just an old family friend who's staying over for a little while.'

'A little more than a friend from the grin on your face, Dr. S!'

'It's just a bit of fun. He'll be heading home soon and that'll be it.'

'Bloody men,' Lily said. 'Love you and leave you. Well, you may as well enjoy it while you can. Where's he from?'

'The Falklands,' I said, mentally scanning the globe for somewhere far and remote.

Lily looked taken aback but before she could respond, Jenny slid into the chair beside me.

'Jessie, I want to know all about that gorgeous guy you were with yesterday. You should see him, Lily, eyes to drown in.'

I drained my coffee and stood. The chair scraped on the linoleum floor. 'Nothing to tell.' I caught the disbelieving look she shot me. 'Really.'

Just to complete the triumvirate, on my way to my wards, Mark lumbered across my path. I wondered what I had ever seen in him. I found myself looking at his receding hairline and his paunch as if seeing him for the first time. I shivered as I remembered the delicious hardness of Nat Preston's stomach beneath my hands....and my lips.

'Dr. Shepherd,' he said, stepping in front of me. 'Mr. West-macott? What can I do for you?'

Now he had my full attention, he seemed to forget what he had intended to ask me. \

He lowered his voice. 'I think I left some things at your house. I meant to collect them yesterday.'

'Oh, you mean your tracksuit bottoms?'

'And a t-shirt I was rather fond of.'

'Oh, those. I gave them to charity,' I said.

As I made to go past him, he grabbed my arm. I looked down at the restraining hand and said in an icy tone, 'Let go, Mark.'

'Who was that guy?'

I glared at him and he released me. 'Just a friend.'

Mark stared at me, his face flushed and breathing shallow. For a moment, I almost felt sorry for him and put my hand on his arm.

'Mark, I'm moving on. Time you did too.'

He gave me a reproachful look as he turned and stomped down the corridor.

---

WHEN I GOT home that evening, Alan and Nat were sitting on my sofa, drinking my beer while Alan tried to explain the rules of cricket to Nat.

Nat stood as I entered.

'Jessie,' he said, sweeping his hand at the sofa. 'Come sit down with us and perhaps you can explain to me what it is about this sport that your brother finds so entrancing?'

'Call yourself an Englishman?' I chided as I plopped down next to him

As his arm slid around my shoulder, Alan cast us both a sideways glance.

'Ah, so that's how it is?' he said, 'Leave you alone for one day, and look what happens. Want a beer, Jess?'

Nat and I looked at each other and smiled. Alan let out a heavy sigh, stood and walked into the kitchen. 'I'll take it as a yes for the beer.'

'Alan let me drive his motor carriage today,' Nat said with a grin.

'Oh, Al, how could you? What if you'd been caught?'

'We went out to the old airfield. Not much harm he could do there,' Alan said from the depths of the refrigerator.

I looked at my lover. 'So, did you enjoy it?'

Nat grinned. 'I believe I reached a speed of twenty miles per hour,' he said. 'Imagine how far I could go in that time!'

'Twenty miles? Were you practicing on one of our motorways?'

Alan chortled but Nat looked from one to other of us. 'Is there some merriment?'

'Our motorways are renowned for their traffic jams,' I said, but seeing the puzzlement in his eyes, shook my head. 'Doesn't matter.'

Undeterred, Nat continued, 'I see you have one of Leonardo's machines in your garage. Can you show me how it works?'

I stared at him blankly. 'One of Leonardo's machines?'

'The contraption with two wheels. We saw the old woman on one.'

'Oh, my bicycle. It's a lady's bike but sure, I'll teach you how to ride it.'

Alan returned with beers for the three of us. 'This weekend is the fair up at Heatherhill Hall. Mortlock's regiment is having a muster to commemorate the Battle of Chesham Bridge. I thought it would be amusing if you could come along, Nat.'

Nat looked at him blankly.

'A muster? What are you mustering?'

'Alan is a member of the local historical re-enactors. They re-enact life in the armies of the English Civil War. A muster is when they get together and put on a demonstration of--' I paused, feeling rather foolish. 'Life during the English Civil War.'

'Why?' Nat asked.

A faint color rose to Alan's cheeks. 'Because we find it particularly interesting,' he said.

'It's not interesting. It is a war,' Nat said. 'The worst of wars--a civil war. I would think it is best forgotten, not, what do you call it, 're-enacted.' Do you kill each other?'

'Of course we don't.' Alan cleared his throat and looked away.

'But they pride themselves on being authentic,' I said. 'That's what convinced Alan of your story. Your clothes.'

'I have--I had--two brothers,' Nat said. 'My youngest brother, Thomas, took up arms for Parliament. He was killed at the battle at Long Marston in Yorkshire last year.'

'Were you there?' I asked.

He shook his head. 'No, but my second brother Edward was. He cannot live with the fact that he could have faced his own brother on the battlefield and not known. That is what a civil war means.'

My hand closed over Nat's.

Alan sighed. 'I'm sorry if you find it offensive, Nat.'

Nat shook his head. 'No. I just find it strange. In fact, it is one of the stranger aspects of your world. Do you find us quaint or are we something to be studied like a barbarian tribe?' He looked at me. 'Or is it just all so long ago that the reality of what the war really means is lost?'

Alan shrugged. 'No, it's about remembering, and not forgetting, that this was the last time war was waged on British soil, and what it meant for the future of the country.'

Nat regarded him for a moment and then gave a self deprecating laugh. 'I will come if only because it will be amusing to see how you 're-enact' my time.'

'I could introduce you as a sort of expert in the period?'

He looked so hopeful, I could not help laughing. 'Alan. You are incorrigible.'

'But he's a firsthand resource, Jess.'

An ironic smile quirked the corner of Nat's mouth. He looked at me. 'Where are my clothes?'

'I sent them to the laundry. I've no idea how to get that much blood out of them and I had to do some fast talking.' I rose to fetch another beer. When I opened the fridge I said, 'I've taken leave for the next two weeks.'

'Leave?' Alan asked. 'I thought that hospital couldn't run without you.'

'Well they weren't happy, particularly at such short notice, but they'll manage. Where do you want to go, Nat?' I asked as I returned to the living room.

'Go?'

'We can go to London, Paris...' I paused. 'Even Rome?'

'But I have such a short time.'

'If you want, we can fly. We can be in Rome in two hours from London.' Nat's jaw dropped. 'Two hours, but it took me months...'

'One small problem, Jess,' Alan said. 'Our friend here has no passport. In fact, he has no birth certificate. He doesn't actually exist. Even in the EU, he still needs some sort of ID.'

My grand plans fell to dust. In a time when identity was everything, Nat's lack of any sort of identification could prove to be a real problem...if he were to stay. My heart leaped at the thought. What if he did stay?

My mind whirled ahead to clandestine meetings with shady forgers capable of whipping up such vital documents in the dark alleys of... Where was I to find shady forgers in the back streets of Northamptonshire?

'It's of no matter,' Nat said with a shrug. 'Can we still go to London? I haven't been there since before the war.'

'We don't need a passport for London,' I said. 'We'll take the train tomorrow and be back for the weekend.'

'Excellent plan. Although you may find it's changed since your time,' Alan said. 'The London you would have known burned down in 1666.'

'I served at the court of King Charles for nearly a year. Is Whitehall Palace still there?' Nat asked.

'No,' Alan said, 'apart from Westminster Hall and the Dining Hall, but Hampton Court and the Tower of London are still recognizable. Sorry, did you say you served at Charles's court?' I could see the possibilities whirling through his academic mind. 'Tell me about it?'

I glanced at my watch. 'Are you staying for dinner, Alan?'

Alan is a good brother and quite capable of taking a hint. He excused himself and I was alone with Nat. We barely made it to the bedroom, and dinner was eaten late.

---

WE STAYED in a little hotel off Piccadilly. We spent the nights making love, ate in small restaurants, drank far too much wine and reveled in each other's company.

I generally avoided London as much as I could but with an eager tourist in tow, I saw it through fresh eyes. He absorbed everything about the city. As Alan had said, the city he had known had long since disappeared but we found places he recognized remaining, such as the Tower of London and Westminster Hall and the Abbey of course. Despite the centuries, these buildings still dominated the city.

As we walked down Whitehall, past what had once been the Whitehall palace, we stopped to admire the great equestrian statue of Charles I and the somber statue of Oliver Cromwell.

'Cromwell,' he said musingly, 'I have heard his name. He is a fine commander of the cavalry I believe. I must ask Alan what he did to warrant such a place of honor.'

'Oh, I can tell you that,' I said and proceeded with a history lesson on Cromwell's rise to being Lord Protector. He listened intently, his expression grim, and made no comment.

We stopped at the modest building that was the last remaining vestige of the great Whitehall Palace, the Dining Hall designed by Inigo Jones, another building apparently known to

Nat. As it was open to the public, I paid our entry and we joined a guided tour.

Nat grew more and more withdrawn as the tour progressed. The guide stood by the windows and described how King Charles I had stepped onto the scaffold on that cold winter's day in 1649 to meet his death. Nat turned away and left the group.

I found him standing on the street outside, leaning against a wall. 'Are you all right?'

'They killed the king,' he said without looking at me,

'Yes, they did. You will need to ask Alan more about it.'

'Everything we are fighting for, everything I will die for will be for nothing.'

'No.' I shook my head. 'No, because of what happened, England will be a better place. The monarch will be accountable for his or her actions to the parliament. There will be no more civil wars.'

'And your queen?' he waved a hand in the direction of Horse Guards. 'Does she rule by divine right?'

'No. She is a figurehead with no real power.' Nat straightened. 'I need a drink.' I took his hand. 'Let's find that drink and then we'll go to the Natural History Museum. I think you will find that far more interesting.'

As we boarded the train at Paddington on Friday afternoon, I wanted to turn and run in the opposite direction. The battle of Chesham Bridge would be in three days time. The thought filled me with foreboding. Sometime before then Nat would return to his time to die too young. As wonderful as our few days in London had been, it was as though I had given someone with a fatal illness their last taste of life.

So he would not see my tears I turned away and looked out of the window at the passing countryside.

## ❧ 5 ❧

# MUSTERING AT HEATHERHILL

'TODAY,' Alice says. 'Are you ready?'

My arm tightens around Jessie the Witch and she sighs in her sleep. 'Alone?'

'No, she will come with you.'

I kiss Jessica's hair. Will she find my world as strange as I find hers? When I die will she be stranded forever between times?

'No, Alice.'

Alice sighs. 'I must talk with her.'

'Then talk to her as I do with you, Alice. Don't ask this of me.'

I hear Alice's skirts rustle as she paces the room. 'I cannot, Nathaniel. She must come with you.'

'How?'

Alice laughs.

So many things I will never understand and that defy logic. I have no choice but to trust her.

I ROLLED over and looked down at my sleeping lover who lay on his back with one arm flung over his head. I knew every inch of his hard, lean body, every scar and blemish. I wanted to hold on to this moment forever, keep him here beside me, but as inexorably as time, I knew he would be leaving me and when he went, I would be heartbroken. A tear trickled down my cheek. I didn't want to let him go back. If I could nail him to this time and place, lock him in this room, I would.

Instead I cooked him breakfast.

Alan had picked up Nat's clean and mended clothes from the laundry and left them at my house. Nat had spent Friday night polishing his boots, belt and baldric but when the morning came he would not wear them.

'I think it a foolish notion, to dress up and pretend you are in times long past. It would be as idiotic as me pretending to be a bowman of Crecy.'

'Oh, there are re-enactment groups who do that too.' I smiled. 'And Romans.'

Nat just rolled his eyes and stowed the bag with his clothes in the boot of my car.

A large crowd had gathered at the Hall. The lady in the pink cardigan, flushed by the exertion of dealing with the number of visitors, greeted us like old friends.

'Back again?' she said. 'We've got the Civil War Association here, you know.'

'Yes, my brother is one of them.'

'And what about you, dear?' she addressed Nat. "Are you getting dressed up too?' she asked, eyeing the sword and boots he carried.

'Of course,' he replied. 'Isn't that the point?'

'Oh...but you've cut your lovely hair.'

Nat ran a hand through his shorn locks and gave her the

benefit of his most disarming smile. 'I am sure the likeness is still there.'

A faint color stained her cheeks and she giggled like a teenager. 'Oh well, I will look out for you,' she said.

We identified Alan by the standard flying above his tent. He looked rather fine in his green jacket and sleeveless buff coat.

Nat shook his head. 'This is some dream from which I will wake,' he said.

'Did you bring your clothes?' Alan's eyes gleamed.

'Of course,' Nat said as he set the bag down on the table. 'And did you find something for Mistress Shepherd?'

'Oh, I'm not getting dressed up. I don't--' But the protests died on my lips as Nat kissed me.

'I would like to see you dressed as a proper woman,' he whispered, cupping my face in his hand.

I batted it away. 'You chauvinist. Do you think long skirts and corsets make me a proper woman?'

'A lady suitable for my arm on this fine day of battle?' Nat wheedled.

I relented, and with some help from a couple of the female 'camp followers,' I entered into the spirit of the day, emerging in a heavy blue wool frock and neat lawn collar trimmed with lace. They could find no shoes to fit me, so I kept my sneakers on.

Nat held out his arm. 'Now we look the part. Like a pair of strolling players.'

'Except they didn't have women actors in your day.'

'True,' he said.

'You look stunning, Jess, although I'm not sure about the handbag,' Alan observed, pointing to my large leather bag, slung over my shoulder.

'I'm not leaving it in a tent.'

Alan shrugged. 'We've got a little time before we kick off. I thought we should go and visit Nat's sword,' he said.

Unlike our previous visit, the great hall was full of tourists. Standing beneath his portrait, even with his hair cut short, there could be no denying Nathaniel Preston was the subject of Van Dyck's portrait. My heart beat a little harder beneath the constricting bodice. Nat unsheathed the shining sword and held it up to the glass case. It was incredible to think it was the same weapon.

'Well, well. That is a superb copy. Do you mind if I have a look?'

We turned to find ourselves face to face with the elderly gentleman dressed in the same tweed jacket we had passed in the woods the first day we had come to Heatherhill.

His gaze was fixed on Nat, who, without a word, presented the sword to him. The gentleman turned it over in his hands. 'A perfect replica, right down to the nick just below the hilt. I commend you, sir. Where did you have it made?'

'Germany,' Nat said.

The man turned to look at the Van Dyck portrait. 'You will pardon my curiosity, but I can't help but notice that you bear a striking resemblance to my ancestor. Are you distantly related to my family?'

'You are a Preston?' I asked, deflecting the question.

'Indeed. Colonel George Preston. The last of the Prestons, alas.' The elderly man indicated the portrait of Nat. 'My ever-so-great grandfather by direct line. One of the dashing cavaliers of King Charles. He died in the Civil War.'

Out of the corner of my eye I saw Nat wince.

The Colonel had not missed the momentary lapse in Nat's composure. 'But you haven't answered my question. Are we related?'

Nat met the eyes of his great-plus grandson. 'Family history is not my interest. I would need to consult my grandmother.'

'Well, I would be most interested to meet with you again, Mr...'

'Preston, Nathaniel Preston,' Nat said with a smile. 'I carry the name, Colonel.'

George Preston's moustache twitched. 'Indeed you do, sir. Well, if you will excuse me, I believe I have the honor of starting a battle. I look forward to our next meeting.' With a slight bow, the military gentleman left us.

'Well, that was an odd conversation,' I remarked.

'Odd,' agreed Alan. 'You would think he knew who Nat was.'

'Yes, but that's not likely is it?' I said. 'Come on, Al, you'll be late.'

'What exactly are you doing today?' Nat asked as we walked toward the line of tents that marked the muster.

'It's supposed to be the battle of Chesham Bridge but we're not blowing anything up.'

'What was blown up?' Nat inquired.

'The bridge, of course,' Alan replied. 'It stopped the Parliamentarians in their tracks and allowed time for the king to bring up more troops. We should use you as our technical advisor for the battle.'

'Alan, may I remind you, Nat hasn't fought the battle of Chesham Bridge yet,' I said and instantly regretted my words.

In two days time, Nat would fight the battle and he would die but he didn't appear to have heard me. He had wandered over to one of the cavalry and was talking to the trooper. In fact, he appeared to be giving the man some advice on his equipment.

Alan introduced him to the gathering as a technical specialist on seventeenth century armament who he had invited along for the day. A trumpet sounded, and the muster assembled.

Nat shuddered. 'I've no stomach to watch this. Come, let's go for a walk to the river.'

We found a gate in the wall and strolled with our arms around each other, through the orchard to the banks of the River Nene, which flowed deep and dark from upstream of Chesham. Nat sat down on the bank. I spread my skirts and sat beside him. We fell back in the sweet smelling grass and I laid my head on his shoulder as he slid his arm around me.

We lay together, listening to the murmur of the river and the distant sound of the battle.

'This is nice,' I whispered, feeling his fingers stroking my hair. 'Let's enjoy it, while we can,' he whispered.

---

I MUST HAVE FALLEN ASLEEP. When I opened my eyes, the sun had slipped away and we were lying in shadow. Despite the heavy woolen clothes, I shivered as a cold breeze blew across the water.

No sound came from the direction of the Hall. The battle must have finished and Alan and his mates would have retired to the beer tents.

I stretched and sat up,

'Alan will be wondering where we are,' I said

Nat brushed the grass from his breeches as he stood up. He held out his hand and pulled me to my feet.

'Have they finished fighting my war?'

I glanced at my watch. The digital face had gone blank. I took it off and shook it, annoyed that the new battery I had just put in it had failed.

Knowing the habits of Alan and his comrades I said, 'They'll all be well into their cups by now.'

'I'm still not sure that I understand why they do it,' Nat said, 'but their attention to detail is impressive.'

He bent down and collected his sword and my handbag. I

slung the incongruous twentieth century handbag across my shoulder as he buckled on his sword.

He took my hand and raised it to his lips.

'Come with me, Jessie. It's time to go back.' He caught my face in his free hand and kissed me. 'Jessie, my witch,' he whispered.

We walked through the orchard, arms around each other. Nat pushed open the door in the wall and stood aside for me to enter.

The moment I stepped through the door I knew that time had turned its circle. I recoiled into Nat's arms, desperately scanning the surroundings for a familiar landmark. The car park had gone and the garden had disappeared. Only the house, basking in the late afternoon sun was still recognizable, except for an additional wing, the missing west wing.

I caught my breath and turned but Nat had closed the door and stood blocking my way. I tried to go around him but he caught my arms, pulling me in close to him.

I struggled in his grip. 'Let me go. I don't belong here. I have to go home.'

He held me firmly by the forearms, looking into my eyes, willing me to trust him. 'You can't go back. Not yet. You are here for a reason. Grandmother was insistent. We must trust her judgment in this.'

I shook his hands off and took a step back, looking at him as the truth of my situation dawned on me. I had been kidnapped and transported to somewhere my family and friends would never find me.

'You knew? You knew when you were returning? You knew all about it?' My accusing words sounded shrill to my own ears.

He ran a hand through his hair. 'Not all of it,' he said. 'Grandmother only told me this morning.'

'But when did you speak to your grandmother?' I stared at him in disbelief.

If his appearance in my garden had turned my world on its head, this new development had shaken me to the core. I wanted to cry, pound my fists against his chest but most of all, I wanted to go home.

He looked away. 'Jessie, you will return to your own time. Trust me.'

I rushed at him, pushing him hard enough for him to take a step away from me. 'I don't want to be here, Nat. I don't want to watch you die.'

As I pushed past him, my hand reaching for the gate, he caught me by the waist. He wrapped his arms around me and kissed my forehead.

'It's too late,' he said. 'The gate is shut. You can't go back.'

'But I must! I don't belong here. This is your time.'

He closed his eyes and took a breath. 'And for a little while you will share it with me.' He tilted my chin up, forcing me to look up at him. He smiled. 'Grandmother will answer your questions in good time. She said she must speak with you.' He released me and held out his hand, palm up. I laid my hand over his and his fingers curled over mine. 'Now, let us make the most of what little time we have. Come and meet my family, Jessica Shepherd.'

## ❧ 6 ❧

# NO SPAGHETTI FOR DINNER

EVEN IF *I had closed my eyes as I shut the door in the orchard wall, I knew I had come home. The smell is different. Jessie the Witch's time smells of the potions that run the motor carriages. Even here in the country it hung like a miasma in the air.*

*Now I can smell the wood smoke from the kitchen and other less pleasing smells from the dog kennels and the farmyard. Strange, that I had never noticed them before. I wonder what else will not sit well with me, now I have seen another time?*

*To begin with, I must explain my polled head.*

*And Jessie the Witch.*

*Her fingers, clasped in mine, tighten as we approach the house, betraying her fear. How do I explain this beautiful woman with her strange speech and stranger ways?*

---

NAT HELD my hand as we walked down a narrow path toward the house. A maid carrying a basket of washing rounded a corner of the house and seeing us, gave a sharp cry, dropping the washing in the dust. The noise drew the attention of the household and we were surrounded by men, women and children all clamoring their welcome to their lost master.

No one spared me a second glance. In my borrowed costume I looked no different from any of the other women. I wrenched my hand free from Nat's, seeing the plan and furious that I had allowed myself to be duped. Knowing he would return today, Nat had contrived to put us into costume. Imagine if I had arrived in his time dressed in my jeans and a t-shirt. I would probably be burned as a witch. I tried to hate him, but failed. At least I blended into the background.

'Nathaniel.' A woman's voice cut through the noise and we all turned to the main door of the house. An elderly woman stood on the top step dressed in a heavy black gown with a stiff ruff around her neck. An old fashioned gown, even for 1645. She raised the cane she carried and brought it down on the stone step with a thud.

'Welcome home, Nathaniel Preston. We have been much worried about you.'

Nat bowed. 'Greetings, Dame Alice.'

Dame Alice, the cause of my current dilemma. I studied my nemesis through narrowed eyes, and she turned to me. Our gazes locked and a whisper, like the rustle of dry leaves, caught in my head.

'Later, Jessica, we will talk later.'

I must have started, as Nat turned to look at me with a frown. Now I was hearing things?

'Come inside. You and your companion must be thirsty from your long journey.'

For the first time the rest of the household turned to me with curious looks. I shifted uncomfortably from one sneaker-clad foot to the other.

Nat looked at me and he caught my hand in his. 'Jessie?'

He smiled at me, his gaze holding mine. He was willing me to trust him, and in all honesty, that was all I could do. I gave a slight nod indicating I understood and would follow his cues.

Dame Alice turned and walked into the building. Nat released my hand and I took a deep breath as we followed her up the strangely familiar steps into Heatherhill Hall.

Nat strode into the great hall and tossed his sword on the table as if he owned it, which of course, he did.

'Fetch us some ale,' he said and took a seat at the head of the long table, his familiar position, I surmised from the familiarity with which he sprawled in it.

I had last seen the great hall full of tourists. It seemed so strange to see it as a part of living household. A servant appeared at Nat's elbow with a jack of ale, and a mug was offered to me. I took it for want of anything else to do, and subsided onto a bench beside Nat, while his retainers gathered around to hear his story. I too waited to hear what logical explanation he would give for his missing week.

Dame Alice sat across the table from me. I felt her watching me and concentrated my attention on the contents of my mug.

'Nathaniel! Thank the Lord you are safe.' A young woman dressed in a green gown with lace-edged collar and cuffs of white linen entered the hall. She crossed the hall and threw her arms around his neck. 'Where have you been? We have been so worried.'

She placed a hand possessively on his shoulder and Nat looked around the table. 'What was the last news you had of me?' he asked.

The young woman spoke again. 'We heard a report that you had been set upon by a party of the enemy. Simmons went looking for you and found your horse shot dead. We have scoured the countryside for news of you and were in despair. '

Nat set his ale down. 'I am sorry to have caused you so much concern. The report was correct. I was pursued by the round-heads and took a wound to my arm. When my horse was shot from beneath me I was forced to run. I feared myself dead, had it not been for the kindness of this woman, Mistress Shepherd, who took me in.' He looked at me. 'I fear I was out of my senses for a few days but she has nursed me back to health.' He smiled at the company and spread his hands in a gesture that encompassed me. 'And now, here we are.'

Conscious that the assembled company was all looking at me, I managed a watery smile.

'Mistress Jessica Shepherd, my grandmother, Dame Alice and my sister, Mary.' Mary gave me a sharp glance and her lip curled in an expression of disdain. Nat patted her hand, and without looking at her, said, 'Take that look off your face, Mary. I assure you Mistress Shepherd is quite the equal of you.'

Mary's eyes narrowed and she turned back to her brother, touching his hair. 'Your hair...' She looked across at me. 'Did you crop it for the fever?'

I scrabbled back in my memory to a history of medicine lecture. It had been a commonly held belief that long hair sapped the patient's strength.

'Err, yes,' I agreed. 'He was taken with wound fever.' And would have been lucky not to die from septicemia, I thought, marveling at how far medicine had come.

'You seem to have made a remarkable recovery,' Mary kissed her brother again. 'Mistress Shepherd, we owe you a debt of gratitude,' the young woman said, although her expression remained wary.

'We are indeed grateful to you, Mistress Shepherd, for restoring Nathaniel to us,' Dame Alice addressed me for the first time.

In all the time I had been in the hall, her gaze had hardly

left me, and now as I looked at her, I saw where Nat had inherited his unusual gray-green eyes. She lowered her voice and said, 'I have heard much about you and have been anxious to meet you.'

I hoped nobody else in the room had overheard us. It would seem a strange thing to say to someone she had apparently only just met. I responded in a soft voice, holding her gaze so she could be under no illusions I was indeed who she thought I was, 'And I you, Dame Alice.'

She nodded and rose to her feet. 'What matters for the moment is that you are both here and safe. Tonight we will dine well. Mary, pray take Mistress Shepherd to the best guest bedchamber and see she has all she needs. Nathaniel, you and I must talk.'

I wanted, more than anything, to have a few words with Dame Alice, but Mary stood by the door waiting for me and I followed her from the great hall. She led me up the wide oak stairs to the west wing, the wing that no longer existed.

MARY SHOWED me to a room that, had it still been in existence in the twentieth century, would be described in a guide book as the green bedroom. The bed had been hung with green woolen curtains and an embroidered cloth covered in carefully worked patches and darns, indicating that it might already have been of some antiquity, covered the sheets.

'Where did you say you were from?' Mary inquired.

'Chesham,' I replied without thinking, and immediately wished I had said Northampton as Mary frowned.

'There are no people by the name of Shepherd in Chesham, and I can tell by your voice and manner you have some gentility in your upbringing.' She looked at me with the same sideways glance her brother used. I found the resemblance a little unnerving.

'My people are from London,' I answered with absolute truth. 'I am but new to Chesham.'

'You could have sent word that Nathaniel was with you,' Mary said in a reproachful tone. 'We have been frantic with worry.'

I had to think fast. 'Being new to the village, I did not know who he was until he recovered sufficient of his senses to inform me.'

That seemed to satisfy her.

'Shall I send someone to fetch your own possessions--that is, if you are staying?' From her raised eyebrow it would seem she suspected my relationship with Nathaniel might be more than just that of nurse and patient.

'No. I'm not staying long. I just came to make sure Nathaniel got back safely.'

Mary sank on to the edge of the bed and looked down at her folded hands. 'Thank you for what you have done for him. We feared the enemy had seized him. I have lost one brother and it would kill me to lose another.'

The breath stopped in my throat. Foreknowledge was a dreadful burden, I realized.

I sat next to her and took her hand. 'This is a terrible war, Mary. I fear there will be many more deaths before it is over.'

A large tear slipped down her cheek and she dashed it away impatiently. 'Has Nathaniel told you about my...my beloved?' I shook my head.

'Robert took up arms for Parliament with our brother, Richard. They had been boon companions since childhood. Now Richard is dead and Robert...' She sniffed, 'I fear I will never see him again.'

I had no knowledge of this relationship and felt grateful for the ignorance, but if Robert survived the war, there stood a good chance that he, being on the winning side, would come for his sweetheart. The family would need such allies in the years to come.

'You and Nathaniel?' she ventured. 'I saw the way he looked at you and I don't understand how such a thing has come to pass in so short a time.'

'Mistress Preston,' I said, remembering my seventeenth-century manners. 'In war, there is no time for the niceties of courtship.'

A smile quirked her lips. 'Well, I am pleased for him, if he has found love at last. Dear Anne, God rest her, was not his equal. They would have made each other very unhappy.' Mary rose and straightened her skirts. 'You must be tired after your long walk from Chesham. I will leave you to get settled. You may stow your sack in the chest.' She indicated my brown leather handbag, which I carried still slung over my shoulder.

With an elegant twitch of her skirts, she left the room

I sat on the edge of the bed and looked down at my sneakers. I wondered what I looked like and if I appeared strange to these people. I could see no mirror in the room, so I unhooked my handbag and scrabbled in it for my small mirror.

The reflection in the tiny glass gave me no reassurance. I might as well have been dropped into the Amazon jungle. As I replaced the mirror, I reflected that if Nat had survived the twentieth century, I would survive the seventeenth. I just hoped I would not be stuck here forever, after he...after he... I screwed my eyes shut, took a deep, steadying breath and tried not to think about Nat's fate.

A firm rap on the door startled me out of my reverie. I jumped to my feet and my handbag went flying, strewing its contents across the wooden floor. Without waiting for a response, Nat entered the room. He looked down on me as I scrabbled under the bed trying to find the stray lipsticks, mints and the inevitable loose change that rattled around in the bottom of my bag.

'That is a tempting sight.' He patted me playfully on my well padded rear end.

I stood and turned to face him. He moved toward me with a smile I had come to recognize. My pulse began to quicken and a warm glow spread through my stomach as he pulled me toward him. 'I can't wait to unlace that bodice,' he whispered. 'And of course, there are other advantages to skirts...'

He slowly pulled up my skirts and ran his fingers along my thigh, leaving a trail of fire. His mouth curled in a smile as he snapped the elastic of my underwear. 'What are you wearing?'

'A good, solid pair of Marks and Spencers best knickers,' I replied, wagging a finger in his face. 'I may know underwear is not in common use for another two hundred years but I am not a complete philistine.'

He laughed and released my skirts. They fell in heavy folds, brushing the tops of my sneakers.

'Later then, Mistress Shepherd, you can demonstrate the virtues of Marks and Spencers best knickers. Now, let me escort you downstairs for supper. My grandmother has ensured a welcome home feast tonight. A lamb has been slaughtered.'

'No spaghetti?'

He smiled. 'No spaghetti.'

---

THE GREAT HALL, lit only by candles, pulsed with chatter and the comings and goings of the servants. Seeing it so alive reminded me this had once been a home, not a museum. Twenty people sat down to eat at the long table, and the presence of the officers of Nat's regiment was a stark reminder this was not just Nat's home but an army garrison now.

I had been to dinners put on by Alan's regiment so I tried to imagine myself among Alan's drinking mates, but found it hard. I had been seated well away from Nat at the far end of the table with the women of the house. In 1645, I inhabited a man's world.

The talk turned to the war, and from the grim look on the men's faces, I concluded the social part of the evening had ended and it was time for the war to recommence.

Dame Alice rose and announced that the ladies would leave the gentlemen to their deliberations. Mary excused herself to retire to her bedchamber and I would have done likewise, but Dame Alice took my arm and steered me into a private parlor. It might have been the black gown or the stiffness of her ruff, but I had no desire to cross Dame Alice.

She shut the door behind her and seated herself in a straight-backed chair, gesturing for at a similar chair. I had imagined Dame Alice as some sort of sorceress from the movies, dressed in flowing robes with a tall, pointed hat, accompanied by a black cat. As I sat across from her, I realized I had not expected a stiff little person in an old fashioned gown--an ordinary woman.

As she seemed in no hurry to speak, I took advantage of her silence to get in first. 'I don't know how you have managed this, Dame Alice, but send us back.'

She raised an iron-gray eyebrow. 'Us?'

'I'm not leaving here without Nat.'

Her implacable countenance did not change. 'Mistress Shepherd, you know Nat's future.'

I slumped in the chair. 'If he stays here he is going to die,' I whispered.

Her face, so like her grandson's in the light of the fire, did not appear to show any emotion but a slight movement of the ruff betrayed a tightening of her throat. This hint of humanity gave me some measure of relief, and I continued. 'I can't change history, Dame Alice. Nat dies in two days and his son inherits the estate. It's written in the books, and it's carved in stone in the chapel.'

She looked up at me. 'Have some patience, Mistress Shepherd. All is not as you think it. You will understand when the time comes.'

I shook my head. 'I don't understand any of it.' Looking up at her, I asked, 'Are you really a witch?'

She frowned and she put a hand to her chest, an expression of alarm on her face. 'If they had the courage, there are some who may call me that, but not to my face. I am just an old woman with some skills in healing. Do not call me a witch in any person's hearing, Mistress Shepherd, or I will be hanged.'

'Sending people through time is not just "some skills in healing". I have some skills in healing. What you have is much more powerful, and I don't profess for a moment to understand it.'

For the first time, a slight smile tugged at the corners of her lips. 'I come from a long line of wise women, Mistress Shepherd. There are some who say we are descended from Nimue, King Arthur's lover. I have a gift, as my mother and my grandmother and theirs had long before me.'

'Has Mary inherited it?'

'No, but it is not confined to the women's line. Nat has snatches of it.'

'Is that why you can move him around in time and talk to him?'

She gave me an inscrutable look and I wasn't going to argue. I had woken that morning in the twentieth century and I would be going to bed in the seventeenth century. Nimue, Merlin, Morgana--it didn't really matter which sorcerer she believed she was descended from. I was too tired to take any more in.

As if reading my thoughts, she stood and put her hand on my

shoulder. 'You have travelled far today, Mistress Shepherd. Go and rest and tomorrow we will talk further. I will send my maid to help you with your clothes.'

At all of five feet, six inches, I seemed to be uncommonly tall for the time and, as I stood, I seemed to tower over Dame Alice. I smoothed down my rumpled skirts and nodded. I would never get out of the combined skirts, petticoats and bodice without someone to help me.

'Good night, Dame Alice,' I said at the door.

'Good night, Mistress Shepherd.'

I left her standing in the middle of the room, a small, still figure in a black dress.

## 7

# MAGIC AND MODERN MEDICINE

*WHEN I FINALLY MAKE MY way to Jessie, I find she has been crying
and I am angry with Alice. I do not understand why she has brought
Jessie with me.*

*As I slip into the bed and take her in my arms, I can hear Alice
tapping at the corners of my mind. I ignore her. Tonight Jessie needs me
and I need her. We have so little time left. Perhaps tomorrow it will all
make more sense.*

---

I WOKE ALONE to the sounds of voices in the courtyard, mingled
with farmyard sounds of lowing cattle and squawking fowls. A
knock on the door startled me and I barely had time to retrieve
my borrowed nightdress before a maid entered the room with a
bowl and a jug.

'The master said you would like water for washing.' She set
the bowl and jug on the table with a pile of cloths beside it.

Toothpaste would have been good too, I thought, running my tongue over my furry teeth.

'Do you wish me to help you to dress?'

I agreed that would be a good idea. It had taken the girl some time to get me out of my clothes the previous night. If she had noticed my strange footwear and unconventional under-wear, she had known it was not her place to make a comment. I just hoped she had the discretion not to spread the story through the kitchen.

As the maid tightened the laces on the bodice, the noise outside the window changed. Trailing the long suffering maid behind me, I crossed the room to look down on the courtyard.

For a moment, I thought I could have been at one of Alan's musters. Below me, soldiers in seventeenth-century clothing were forming in ranks. I almost expected Alan in his green coat to come striding self-importantly from the house. But this was real, this was war.

At first I couldn't see Nat and then realized he wore a wide brimmed hat with a curling red feather. He looked up at the window, as if sensed I was watching. I raised my hand and he smiled, his fingers going to the brim of his hat in an informal salute.

The maid coaxed me back from the window and sat me on a stool while she attacked my hair. She proved more adept than the twentieth-century camp followers the previous day, and managed to coax it into some sort of bun-like arrangement coiled at my nape with long, curling strands framing my face. I quite liked the effect, or what I could see of it, in my tiny mirror.

When she was finished and had excused herself, I pulled the stool to the window and sat with my chin on my hand, watching the activity in the courtyard.

'Nathaniel will see you later this morning.' Dame Alice's voice made me jump. I stood and turned to face her.

'Is that another prognostication?' I inquired.

She smiled. 'No, he gave me the message. He said there is something he wishes to show you. Until then, perhaps you would care to come with me. You may be interested in my potions and herbs. I really do have some skills in healing and you, as a practitioner of the healing art, may find my receipt book of some interest.'

'Receipt book?'

Alice frowned. 'The book where I record the ingredients and the method of making my unguents.'

'Oh...a recipe book.'

Alice just gave me a puzzled glance.

'Are you going to tell me how you know who I am?' I asked as I followed her through the maze of stairs and corridors.

'In good time, Mistress Shepherd,' she replied, stopping to unlock and open the door to what she called her still-room.

She stood back to allow me to enter first. Bunches of drying herbs hung from hooks and little round clay pots crammed the shelves between stoppered flagons. My nose twitched. The room smelled of sage and rosemary with the tinge of something sweet, such as honey. We had touched on the history of medicine in my studies and here was an opportunity to study it at firsthand. My professional curiosity overcame any reservations I may have had about Dame Alice.

'This is extraordinary,' I said.

She shut the door behind her and indicated a heavy, leather bound volume on the table. 'That is my book of receipts. The sum total of my knowledge.' She looked up at me with her grandson's clear eyes. 'It would be wonderful to be born in your time, to have your knowledge.'

'What do you know of my time?' I challenged.

'What I have seen, Doctor Shepherd. Extraordinary machines that do the work of men and horses. Magic lights and water that comes from the walls, but I have also seen unhappiness and poverty. Those things are universal to any age.'

'How do you see?' I looked around the room, wondering if she kept a crystal ball or some sort of bowl with magical divining liquid in it.

She touched her eyes. 'I see these things when I close my eyes,' she said.

'Did Nat know what you intended for him?'

She tilted her head to one side. 'We discussed it at length.'

I pondered that revelation and the duplicity of my lover.

'Why me?'

'You are linked to the cottage.'

My heart skipped a beat. I had been right. This was not about me, it was about the cottage.

'I only bought it eighteen months ago. How can I possibly be linked to it?'

'All things are connected in one way or another, and the cottage has properties that allow it to sit on either side of time.'

'I knew it!'

Dame Alice turned her compelling gaze to me again. 'It is not what you are thinking. It was not just the cottage. I have been waiting for you.'

I frowned. 'You knew I would buy the cottage?'

She gave me that inscrutable smile.

'If you know the future, then you know what is to happen to Nathaniel.' My chest tightened and the first glimmer of hope sprang in me. 'Is there a plan? Can we save him? Is that why you have brought me here?'

'So many questions, Mistress Shepherd. All in good time.' I think, from the little half smile, she enjoyed being mysterious. 'For now, I would like to talk to you about your healing arts.'

Despite the fact she had turned my world upside down, sent me a man to fall in love with--a man with a death sentence--dragged me across three centuries and seemed to revel in being mysterious, I liked Dame Alice. I saw the same hunger for knowledge in her as I saw in her grandson. She, like him, did not belong in this time. While he might have become machine-mad, Dame Alice would have made a fine doctor. She quizzed me extensively about the body and disease. At a time when the circulation of blood had only just been explained, the concept of unseen microbes and germs would have flummoxed anyone other than this extraordinary woman.

We were so engrossed, we did not hear the door open and it was only when Nat said, 'It is pleasing to see the two of you so deep in conversation,' that we looked up.

'Nathaniel, you should knock,' his grandmother reproved him.

'I did. And now if you can spare Jessie for a short time, I would like to borrow her.'

I rose from the uncomfortable stool on which I had been sitting and excused myself. In the doorway, Nat spanned by corseted waist with his hands and kissed me

'Your grandmother...' I mumbled, conscious of Dame Alice's presence in the room behind me.

'Oh, don't mind Grandam,' Nat responded. 'She knows about us.'

I had an uncomfortable feeling that Dame Alice had some kind of seventeenth century closed circuit TV installed in my cottage. Who knew what she had seen? 'I know, but still--'

He cut me off again with a kiss.

'Go, both of you,' Dame Alice said. 'You know I find young lovers tedious.' 'Where are we going?' I asked as Nat shut the door to Dame Alice's still room. 'I want you to meet my sons, the center of my universe,' he replied.

NAT LED me to a room that had not been part of the twentieth-century tour of the house. Beyond the closed door, I could hear children's voices.

He turned to look at me, his face grave. 'I would like you to look at Christian and tell me what ails him.'

'Is he sick?'

He swallowed and nodded. 'He has never been strong and the doctors tell me that he will not live to manhood. We have searched for a healer who may provide us with the answer we seek.'

I stared at him, seeing the grief in his eyes for the child that seventeenth century medicine could not save.

'Is this why I have been brought here?'

He took a breath before he replied. 'I would be easier knowing there is nothing I could have done that could change his fate.'

Nothing he could have done? This father had travelled three hundred years to find the answer to that question.

I took his hand, giving it a small squeeze before Nat opened the door to be greeted with shrieks of delight as two small children, hampered by long skirts, hurtled across the floor. Nat went down on his knees and gathered them to him, kissing their soft curls.

'Why are they wearing skirts?' I asked.

He looked up at me with surprise. 'Because boys are not breeched until they are at least five years old.'

He disentangled the children and rose to his feet. With his hands on two small auburn heads, he turned the boys toward me. 'Boys, I would like you to meet Mistress Shepherd. Now remember your manners.'

I smiled as the two tots executed wobbly bows, made even more bizarre by their heavy skirts.

'This is Nathaniel,' he tapped the shoulder of the taller and stronger boy, 'and this is Christian, the eldest.'

I didn't need to examine Christian to diagnose his symptoms. He was smaller than his twin and thin to the point of emaciation. His pallor and the slight blue tinge to his lips were all I needed. My heart sank.

I greeted the boys with my professional cheerfulness and allowed myself to be shown their wooden Noah's ark. Their father played with them on the floor while I spoke to their nursemaid.

'The little one, Christian,' I said. 'Does he have trouble eating or playing?'

She eyed me suspiciously. 'Aye, but it's not my fault. He gets same as Master Nathaniel.'

I shook my head. 'I'm not blaming you for anything. I have some skill with healing and his father asked me to look at him.'

A stethoscope would have been useful but I made do by pressing my ear against the little boy's frail chest. He giggled and squirmed but when his father told him to be still, he obeyed without question. Even without my reliable modern technology I heard enough to confirm my diagnosis.

When I had finished, I smiled at the child, unable to look at Nat and see the question in his eyes. 'All done. You've been a good boy, Christian. How about a story?'

Nat sat down in a large oak chair and pulled Christian onto his knee. Little Nathaniel, the boy who would grow up to become a confidante of Charles the Second, scrambled up on mine and I wrapped my arms around his warm, well-clothed body and recounted the story of Peter Rabbit in Mr. McGregor's garden. The boys listened with rapt attention and out of the corner of my eye, I could see the nursemaid had stopped her chores to listen as well. I am not the best story teller in the world, but the tale is timeless.

When I was done, Nat stood up and kissed both boys.

'I will be back later,' he said in answer to their cries of disappointment.

I hugged the children and followed their father from the room and down the stairs to another room I hadn't seen in any tour of the house.

'My study,' he explained, and gestured at the bookcase. 'My books.'

He walked to the window and stood with his hands behind his back, looking over the garden.

'Well?' he demanded, turning back to face me.

'He has a hole in his heart, Nat. He was born with it and your doctors are right, it will kill him before he reaches adulthood.'

His shoulders and I threw my arms around him, holding him close, pressing my face into the wool of his jacket.

'There is nothing you could do to change that. Even in our time, it would be major surgery.'

'But in your time, you could save him?'

'Without further investigation with ultrasound and echocardiography it is impossible to know exactly what the abnormality is, Nat. Sorry I can't be more specific.'

He turned back to the window with his back to me and leaned on the windowsill, his head lowered.

'I am going to die tomorrow, Jessie. When I ride away from here, I will never see those two boys again and they will never see me. Nathaniel will grow up without his father. I won't be there to comfort him when Christian dies and even without the knowledge of what you have just told me, I know Christian will die because Nathaniel inherits the estate. You've seen his portrait.'

'Has this always been about Christian?'

He nodded. 'I...we...Alice and...We have been searching through time...we hoped if we found the right person, there may be something that could be done.'

'All I can do is give your family ideas to make his life more comfortable, but without an operation he does not have long.'

'Can you do this operation?'

I looked around. I was in the seventeenth century. I may as well have been in the darkest jungles of Brazil. I shook my head. 'No. It is a complex procedure, Nat.'

He thumped a fist into the windowsill.

I didn't move. I couldn't. His grief went too deep for what comfort I could offer. I had given parents bad news so many times but always with the calm dispassion of a professional. This time I could feel my own heart breaking. A beloved child would die but before then the child would see his father's death.

I turned away from him, sinking into a chair and stifling a sob that rose unbidden. Now I held two lives in my hands. One I could not save, the other I could but not here, not in 1645. As a doctor, I felt utterly helpless. As surely as I knew Nat would die at the battle of Chesham, I knew nothing in the seventeenth century could save Christian.

Tears stung my eyes. It had always been there, the knowledge of his death, but back in 1995 it had seemed like a fantasy. Here it was reality. Outside the house, real soldiers, with real weapons rehearsed for a battle that was to come. Nat may as well have been a man on death row, awaiting execution. He would die, leaving a child living his own death sentence.

For a long moment the grief overwhelmed me. I could do nothing, not even cry. I began to shake with the pent-up emotion. I choked back a sob and Nat raised his head. He turned to me and gathered me up from the chair, folding me in his arms.

'I could change it,' he whispered. 'I could refuse to go.'

I shook my head, knowing, without really being able to explain it logically, that it could not be changed. I pushed away from him and stood holding his hands, my face wet with tears I didn't even know I had shed.

I found my voice and said in a voice that shook with emotion, 'You know you can't, Nat. Fate will catch you--if not tomorrow then on the field at Naseby.'

Nat made a cutting gesture with his hand. 'Enough, Jessie. We can talk later. There is one more thing I have to show you.'

He crossed to a heavy oaken chest, unlocked it with a key he retrieved from behind the books in the case and took out a second box, bound with heavy metal bands. He lifted out a large rectangular bundle wrapped in a soft leather cloth. Laying it on the table he reverently peeled the layers back to reveal a large, leather bound volume that even in 1645 smelt old and musty.

I gasped as he turned the pages, recognizing the unmistakable hand in the fine pen drawings.

'Da Vinci! It's real? In my time it would be worth a fortune.'

He raised an eyebrow and looked at me for a moment before he spoke. 'I found it on a street stall in Florence and had to haggle hard for it, but in truth, I would have paid twice what the man wanted.' He pointed to a drawing that resembled a modern bicycle.

'I tried to make this. Flying machines, war machines...truly Da Vinci had the gift of foresight.'

We were interrupted in our study of Da Vinci's fantastical drawings by rapping on the door.

'Colonel, the patrol is back,' said a man's voice from behind the closed door.

Nat straightened, the soldier once more. 'If I am correct, I will be told that the enemy is approaching from the north. My orders are to prevent them reaching Northampton.' He gave me a lopsided smile. 'To do that, I must deny them Chesham Bridge.'

There it was. His fate lay between us, a dead, unspoken weight in the air.

'Nat...' My voice died. I didn't know what to say. I couldn't prevent what was to happen. I couldn't change history.

## ❧ 8 ❧

# THE BATTLE OF CHESHAM BRIDGE

*I* STAND *by the window and watch the familiar scenes of my life. Above the horizon there is the faintest lightness in the sky, the slight purpling that heralds a warm day but the air is heavy as if God himself presages my fate.*

*Already the servants are astir. I can hear their voices rising from the kitchen block and young May, the dairymaid, crosses the courtyard, still rubbing the sleep from her eyes. I can see lights in the barn where my men are making their preparations. We will ride within the hour.*

*I dare not turn around and look at the woman asleep on the bed. Jessie, my witch. If I close my eyes I can see the round softness of her shoulders and the honey-gold hair that lies tangled around her face.*

*Somewhere in the house my grandmother paces the floor.*

*'Alice, you have told me to trust you, but I am afraid I will never see her again.'*

*She sighs. 'Nathaniel, trust in me, trust in God.'*

*I smile. 'I'm not sure God approves of your work here, Grandam.'*

*'I will answer to him in good time. You understand now, what is to happen?' I incline my head. 'Yes. I can see your purpose. Make it so.'*

I JOINED THE HOUSEHOLD, which had gathered in the great hall to bid the troops farewell. An air of expectancy hung over the room like a pall. Nat entered, tall and straight, dressed much as I had seen him on our first meeting, only this time it seemed right. I was the odd one out.

He moved easily, familiar with the heavy clothes, a sleeveless buff leather coat his only protection against what was to come. His metal breastplate hangs in a glass case in the twenty-first century.

He must not have been wearing it at the time of his... at the time he... today.

He gave his orders to his officers and then turned to his family. He took time with each one: Mary, Dame Alice. When he reached the two little boys he went down on his knees and held them so close they began to squirm. He rose and turned to me and I saw the indecision in his eyes. All he had to do would be to stay here, let the parliamentarian force cross the bridge at Chesham. Would history be changed by all that much? Probably not.

But I knew in my heart the words I had uttered yesterday were true. He could not evade his fate. It was written in stone in a little chapel.

Nat took my hands, and tears pricked my eyes. He laid a finger against my lips and shook his head. Taking my face between his hands, he bent his head and kissed me--a lingering, loving kiss that left me breathless. The strength and tenderness in his hands stopped the very breath in my throat. He stood back and put a finger under my chin, smiled and without a word, turned and walked from the room.

A noiseless sob shook my shoulders. I wanted nothing more than to turn and run to my bedchamber, throw myself on the bed and howl but I was conscious that I was the center of attention and had to maintain decorum.

Mary, standing beside me, turned to face me. I saw no warmth or sympathy in her face as she demanded in a low voice, 'Who are you? What is your business with my brother?'

All I could do was shake my head. If I had tried to speak, I would have dissolved into tears on the spot.

Dame Alice touched her granddaughter on the arm. 'Peace, Mary. Take the little ones outside to wave their father farewell.'

Mary looked from me to her grandmother, a puzzled frown creasing her forehead. She squared her shoulders and took the children by the hand.

With a last suspicious glance at me, she said, 'Come. Let us go and wave to Papa and the brave soldiers.'

Dame Alice and I were alone in the great hall.

A choking sob escaped and I felt Dame Alice's hand on my shoulder. 'Come to my stillroom. You and I must talk.'

In the privacy of Dame Alice's lair, I slumped onto a low stool and buried my head in my hands, trying to hold back the tears.

'Save your tears, Mistress Shepherd. They will not be necessary.'

I looked up at her. 'What do you mean? Nat isn't going to die today?'

'This has never been about Nathaniel,' Dame Alice said. 'You have confirmed what we have long suspected. Christian will not survive his childhood.' Her chin came up. 'Children die. That is a fact of our life, Mistress Shepherd, but in your time he can be saved. That is what you told Nathaniel. Am I right?'

I nodded.

'I have the gift of foresight, Mistress Shepherd. I had seen Nathaniel's fate so we agreed that, when the time was right, I would send him forward to find the cure for his son.'

I blinked. 'And if he didn't, or couldn't, come back, then what?'

She shrugged. 'A victim of our terrible war. But he did come back and he brought you with him. This is meant to be, Mistress Shepherd.'

'What do you mean?'

'I can send you back to your time but I ask you to take the boy with you.' I stiffened, and she continued.

'I understand the enormity of this boon. We are asking you to love Nathaniel's son as if he were your own.'

'But...but...' My protests died on my lips. If I refused then the child would die and Nat's death would be in vain.

'What do I have to do?'

'In the stable, there is a horse saddled and ready for you. We have told Christian's nurse that the child will leave with you and she has packed a bag for him. She thinks you are taking him to London.'

'Where are we going?' 'To Chesham.'

My mouth fell open. Chesham was the last place on this earth I wanted to go, today of all days.

'No, I can't. I don't want to see Nat...I couldn't...' I couldn't watch my lover die. The tears I had been fighting back began to trickle down my face.

Dame Alice raised her hand to still my protests. 'For an intelligent woman, Mistress Shepherd, you can be remarkably dull. I am giving you a chance to save two lives.'

I dashed at my damp face with the sleeve of my gown. 'You mean Nat? How?'

She shook her head. 'That is up to you.' She smiled. 'I assume you can ride a horse?'

'Yes,' I replied with a quaver of uncertainty in my voice.

'Then, go. They are waiting for you at the stable.'

As I turned to leave, she said, 'One last thing, Mistress Shepherd. Nathaniel does not expect you to support his child without his help.'

'I have money.'

'Jessica, he is a proud man. How long do you think he will accept your charity?'

'It won't be charity.'

She shook her head. 'No. Nathaniel and I have discussed the matter and we will make provision for the child.'

'You're going to leave a pot of gold on my kitchen table?' I asked.

'No, under your hearthstone,' Dame Alice replied.

'My hearthstone?'

'You have wondered why the cottage is so important?'

I stared at her. 'There are three hundred and fifty years of occupation between today and my time. Whatever you leave is sure to be found.'

She just smiled. 'Does it look as if your hearthstone has ever been moved?' I shook my head.

'Well then, trust me. Now, Jessica, you must go. Godspeed.'

---

AT THE STABLES I found Christian and his nurse standing beside a stable boy who held the reins of an elderly, dapple-gray mare. The nursemaid held Christian close and I could see she had been crying.

'You'll take good care of him?' she exhorted me as I swung myself into the saddle and arranged the bunched skirts as best I could, slinging my handbag across my back. I held out my arms for the child, wondering how I would manage a horse and a wriggly two-year-old, but Christian came to me meekly.

I encircled him with my arms and he looked up at me with

wisdom beyond his years in his eyes. The same color as his father's eyes.

'We're going on a long journey, Christian,' I whispered. He curled against me and stuck his thumb in his mouth.

The maid sniffed. 'I've put his things in the saddlebag, ma'am. His favorite wooden horse...' She trailed off and the tears ran unchecked down her cheeks.

I leaned down and put a hand on her shoulder. 'I'll take good care of him, as you have done.'

The stable boy handed me the reins and I put my heels to the horse. Of course I knew how to ride. I had been through my 'horsey' phase as a teenager but it had been many years. I hoped I would recall the basics as I urged it forward. The little animal proved to be biddable and responded to my touch.

As I looked back at the house, I saw Dame Alice standing on the doorstep. She raised her hand and I inclined my head, hoping against all things logical that her power would not fail her today.

Keeping a grip on the child made the short journey by necessity, slow. I picked my way through countryside bearing no relation to twentieth-century Northamptonshire and I trusted to my instinct alone that we were on the road to Chesham. Relief flooded me as I saw the familiar church spire of St. Matthews rising above the trees.

As I turned down the lane toward the river, I gave an involuntary cry as I recognized my cottage, still readily identifiable, although somewhat more rustic than its modern incarnation. The same weathered stone wall ran along the lane. Smoke curled from the chimney and chickens picked through the refuse in the yard that would become my garden in three hundred and fifty years.

I turned the pony off the laneway into the woodlands running down to the river. I knew the place that would give me the best vantage point to see the bridge and the village and wait for whatever would happen next.

I dismounted from the pony and lifted Christian down. He looked up at me with his large, trusting eyes and my heart shattered into pieces. I had saved the lives of many children but this one demanded my love and I knew in that instant he had it, completely and unconditionally, as if he had been my own child. I found a flask containing some sort of ale, a couple of apples and a large piece of pie in the saddlebag.

'Horsey?' Christian asked and I found the little wooden animal and gave it to him.

He sat with a thump, his bottom well padded by his heavy skirts. A funny little bundle of boy, I mused, as I spread my skirts, laid out our picnic and sat beside him to wait.

Wait for what?

Above me dark clouds had begun to gather, foreshadowing a storm within the hour. I drew back under the shelter of a large oak tree and hoped the rain would not be too heavy. Umbrellas were yet to be invented and we were likely to get soaked.

From my vantage point, I could see the bulk of Nat's men lined up on the far side of the river. A smaller reserve would be on this side of the river. Their voices carried across the water and I scanned the ranks, seeing Nat's wide-brimmed hat with its distinctive feather. A tall man for his time, I might have known he would have been at the front and center of his men. Why wasn't he wearing a helmet? Had foreknowledge made him careless of his life?

The enemy was out of my line of sight but I sensed from the tense alertness of Nat's troops, they were not far away.

The parliamentarian forces fired the first sally and several of Nat's men crumpled and fell. A wounded man screamed in agony. All my instincts as a doctor cried out for me to help but I knew I could not interfere. I didn't exist in this time and my priority played beside me, making little neighing noises, impervious to the sound of battle.

Some part of me had thought the battle of Chesham Bridge would be just like one of Alan's musters. How could I have been so naive? I hope never to see a real battle again.

A mighty yell went up, and for the first time, I saw the red-coated soldiers as they bore down on the thin line of Nat's men. I knew from Alan's account of the battle Nat's men were outnumbered three to one. In the cold light of the twenty-first century, that was just a number. In the fading light of a summer day in 1645, it meant everything.

The parliamentarians hit the line with a palpable thump. Above the inhuman screams and yelling, the battlefield faded in a haze of smoke from the muskets. I jumped to my feet, desperate to keep that red feather within my sight, but it had disappeared.

Christian looked up at me and began to cry. I picked him up and held him close, whispering quietudes in his ear as he sobbed into my shoulder. All the while, I was scanning the far bank for a sight of Nat.

His men broke, running across the bridge toward the village. I saw Nat, bareheaded now, leap onto the parapet of the bridge and urge his men to the safety of the pre-prepared defensive positions on the village side of the bridge. Hard on their heels, galloping horsemen cut the men down as they turned to run.

Nat didn't move. My arms tightened on the child, I wanted to scream at Nat to run, to hide, to save himself. Not until the last of his men had crossed did he jump down and begin to run.

'Now!' I heard his command as a single shot rang out from the far side of the river.

Nat checked his stride, stumbled and fell to his knees.

I gave an involuntary cry, my heart jumping to my throat, tears already streaming down my face as Nat regained his feet.

The first of the parliamentarians reached the bridge. Without looking backward, Nat hurled his sword across the span of the bridge in front of him. The world around me disintegrated in a succession of explosions that lit the darkening sky. Chesham Bridge collapsed into the River Nene.

The force of the explosion knocked me to the ground and I huddled under the tree, curling around Christian to protect him from the shower of debris that reached as far as us. As history had related, Nat had mined the bridge. Had he also sacrificed himself in the attempt? Without daring to raise my head, I heard shouts, the whinnying of horses, screams from wounded men and the rattle of musket fire.

Christian howled. Without moving, I cradled him as he sobbed inconsolably. I could feel my own tears running down my cheeks and splashing onto his soft curls.

## ❦ 9 ❦

## BACK FROM THE PAST

*THE WATER DRAGS me down in my heavy clothes and my lungs feel as if they will burst. All I have to do is let go of the slender thread of life, but I don't want to die. I have been living with the thought of my death for so long, now I know it can be defeated. I will not die, not today.*

*I strike out and break the surface, taking a deep lungful of air with a grateful prayer to God who had spared me. The river has carried me downstream. I look back and see the shattered bridge rising above the river like a gap-toothed old man. I just need the strength to strike out for the bank and pray that Jessie the Witch finds me before it is too late.*

---

THE RAIN BEGAN, first as the odd drop and then a summer downpour, soaking my heavy clothes. I raised my head as the exultant cries of Nat's men told me I was still in 1645.

Christian had stopped crying and I stood up, settling the child on to my hip. Hardly daring to think of what I would find I walked to the river bank with a heavy heart. If it hadn't been for the child in my arms, I probably would have thrown myself on the grass and given into my grief. For all Alice's fine words, Nat could not have survived the explosion.

The familiar bridge across the Nene lay upstream, its middle span now a gaping hole. Across the river, the red-coated soldiers had pulled back a little distance, leaving the broken bodies of the dead and wounded lying on the ground before the bridge. My doctor's instinct tugged at me again but I had a two-year-old child in my care and at best, I hoped, a wounded man of my own to find.

I did not have to go far. He lay face down in the flattened grass on a curve of the river about fifty yards downstream from where I had been sitting.

'Papa?' Christian pointed at the bedraggled figure.

I set the boy, still holding his precious horse, on the ground.

'You stay here, Christian. Don't move. Okay?'

He gave me a quizzical look. I don't think he understood my strange speech patterns but he did as he was told.

Dreading what I might find, I knelt beside Nat, and with professional efficiency, turned him over. His eyes were closed, his face deathly pale. Swallowing hard, I stilled my breathing and pressed my fingers to the pulse in his neck. Faint but still beating. An involuntary sob of sheer relief escaped my lips.

Now my training as a doctor took over. I knew he had been hit by the musket ball but in the rain, and with the risk of discovery by either side, I could not even begin to examine him. I bent my head and kissed his forehead. It was icy beneath my lips and my Sleeping Beauty did not wake to my kiss.

Instead I patted his face--hard.

'Nat! Wake up. I have to get you home.'

His eyes fluttered and a slow smile tugged at the corners of his mouth. 'I might have known. Jessica, my witch.'

'Where are you hurt?'

'Leg,' he murmured. 'Sweet Jesu, it hurts.' Fully conscious now, he grasped my forearm. 'Do you have Christian with you?'

I nodded.

'Then go, go now. You must get over the wall.'

'The wall?'

'Your wall...your garden wall. That first day...' he grimaced as he tried to move his leg. 'Not much time. Go!'

'Not without you.' Even as I spoke, I tugged at his right arm and placed it across my shoulder.

Despite his protests, and with a supreme effort, I got him standing. I held out my other hand. 'Christian, come with me.'

The little boy took my hand, and we made a strange procession, staggering through the woods to the lane, still the narrow little dirt track down which I had ridden only a few hours earlier.

Mercifully, the lane was deserted, and we reached the wall to what would become my garden. It was too high for me to manage alone. Bracing himself against the stonework, Nat cupped his hands and lifted me so I sat astride the wall. He lifted Christian up to me and I put out my hand.

'You're coming too,' I said.

He shook his head, grimacing in pain as he took his weight on his injured leg. 'Jessie, I can't...'

'Yes, you can. If you stay here you are going to die. I'm not sure how, probably blood loss or gangrene or something horrible. You must come with me, Nat.'

He looked up at me and a smile lifted the corners of his mouth. With an effort that must have taken every last bit of his strength, he hauled himself to the top of wall. With my hand firmly bunched in his collar and one arm around Christian, the three of us tumbled into the garden, ruining what was left of my dahlias.

For a long moment I lay winded in the garden bed with Nat's

dead weight on top of me. Christian had crawled a short distance away and sat on the grass, his horsey in one hand, wailing as if his heart would break.

As I looked toward the cottage, Alan flung open the kitchen door and stood framed in the doorway. I carefully pushed Nat off me and he rolled onto his back with a groan.

I sat up and, gathered the crying child into my arms. 'It's all right, Christian,' I told him. 'We're home now. We're safe.'

And my choking sobs joined Christian's howls.

Alan just stared and I could hardly blame him. His sister, the calm professional, always in control of the situation couldn't move. I sat in a flower bed in a sea of damp skirts, my sneaker clad feet sticking straight out and a crying child clasped in my arms.

For the first time in my life I had to leave it to Alan to sort out the mess.

Nat's fingers found mine. 'Jessie. You're not the one with a musket ball in the leg. For the love of our dear Lord, dry your eyes.'

Alan recovered from his shock and ran across the grass toward us. He looked down at me. 'Are you hurt?'

Jerking my head in the direction of my lover who lay quite still among the broken dahlias, I managed to choke out 'Nat...'

Alan bent over and felt for Nat's pulse. He glanced up at me, a thousand questions in his expression. Questions that would have to wait.

'We've got to get him to hospital, Jess,' Alan said.

Not dressed like this.' My wits had begun to return. 'Get him to the cottage, Alan, and we'll see how bad it is.'

Between the two of us, we managed to manhandle the half-conscious man to the cottage. Christian trailed after us. He looked almost as pale as his father and his breathing sounded ragged, but the little boy's plight was less urgent than his father's.

I sat the child on the sofa, wrapped in a knee rug, from where he watched us with large, round eyes, his thumb in his mouth, as we laid Nat on the hearth. In the harsh glare of the electric light, I saw with a sinking heart that beneath the stubble on his face he was ashen.

'Whisky?' Alan suggested unhelpfully.

'You can pour me one,' I said.

'And me,' Nat said, his eyes fluttering open.

Alan pulled off Nat's boots provoking what I took to be seventeenth century profanities. I found a pair of scissors and cut away the heavy woolen cloth of his breeches.

The musket ball appeared to be lodged in his thigh, but in the absence of a scan, I had no idea how much damage had been done or exactly where the ball had lodged. I pulled the cloth from my coffee table, folded it into a pad and laid it over the wound, which had begun to bleed again with my probing.

'Press on that,' I ordered my brother. Alan complied and Nat swore again.

'What are we going to do?' Alan looked at me, his brow furrowed with concern. I sat back on my heels and shook my head.

'We can't go to the hospital. Gunshot wounds have to be reported. There will be questions asked we can't answer.'

'You will have to use your own skills, Doctor Shepherd.' Nat shook off Alan's hand and pulled himself up so he sat with his back against the sofa.

Alan went to wash his hands and returned with a tumbler of whisky. Nat took a hearty swill of the amber liquid.

'Alan! He could be going under general anesthetic...' I protested.

Alan shook his head. 'No, he's right, Jess. You're going to

have to patch him up yourself. He has no NHS history and a gunshot wound. Questions will be asked.'

I stared at my brother. 'I'm a children's doctor. I don't have the right equipment. It's unhygienic...'

Nat turned his head to look up at Christian, sitting on the sofa above him. 'He shouldn't see me like this. I need you to look after him, not me.'

'Well, you shouldn't have got yourself shot.'

He cast me a cold glance. 'I can wait. Please settle the child first. Then you can find your bag of magic...'

He closed his eyes and took another gulp of the whisky and I turned to Christian. The boy in his strange clothes stared up at me with his large, knowing eyes. I had nothing suitable for a child anywhere in this house.

'Alan, three doors away in Myrtle Cottage, Janice has three children. Please, can you go and knock on her door? Tell her I've got unexpected visitors who've lost their luggage and they have a two-year-old child. I need nappies and clothes.'

Alan nodded and rose. He glanced at Christian with his long curls and skirts and frowned.

'Boy or girl?'

'Boy.'

It is definitely a blessing to have a brother who is a student of the seventeenth century. He accepted my answer without question.

While he was gone, I fed Christian baked beans on toast and a mashed banana. He pulled faces at the strange, unfamiliar food, but to his credit, managed to get most of it down. As I warmed some milk, Alan returned.

I took Christian and the pile of clothes and nappies Janice had provided up to the bathroom. I contemplated running a bath, but didn't want to frighten the child with too many strange experiences on his first night. Instead I washed him thoroughly, dressed him in a nappy and overlarge one piece terry toweling thing with feet in it and carried him downstairs.

Janice, bless her, had provided one of those childproof cups with a spout. I filled it with the warm milk and with an overenthusiastic, 'Say goodnight to Daddy,' carried the boy up to the guest bed room, where I settled him into bed with his horsey.

I lingered a little while to see that he went to sleep but the thought of his injured father downstairs stopped me from sitting with him and singing the lullabies of my childhood. Fortunately, the poor child must have been exhausted. His eyes closed and he was asleep within minutes. I looked down at his innocent little face and took a deep breath.

Now I had to see to his father.

---

I TOOK a few minutes to extricate myself from my seventeenth-century clothes, and clean my teeth. I found a clean, but unsterilized, set of surgical scrubs in my cupboard and after the constricting garments I had been wearing for the last few days, I let out a sigh of relief as I pulled the inelegant garment over my head.

In my medical supplies, I located some basic surgical instruments, sterilized gloves and wipes. They would have to do.

Downstairs, I found Nat had finished off the glass of whisky and a second glass as well. He stared into the empty tumbler with a glazed look on his face.

I rounded on my brother. 'Alan, what were you thinking?'

Alan shrugged. 'Kills the pain?'

'Can't feel a thing,' Nat's voice sounded slurred.

I scrubbed the kitchen table and laid it with clean towels and sheets while the surgical instruments boiled on the stove. I thought of the surgical tents I had seen at Alan's musters. In

Nat's time there would have been no adherence to cleanliness and yet men had survived the brutal, primitive surgery. Modern medicine underestimates the resilience of the human body.

I had no anesthetic except a local, which seemed rather ineffectual given the extent of his injury, but I gave it to him anyway. The whisky may have been more effective. With Alan providing brute force, I did what needed to be done. Somehow the musket ball had managed to miss the major blood vessels and the femur. He had been lucky but I still had to ensure that I removed every shred of cloth and dirt before I dared close the wound.

As I began to probe for the musket ball, Nat fainted and did not come around until after I had finished at which point the whisky took its toll and he was violently ill into a basin. I administered a good shot of penicillin and kissed his clammy forehead.

'I knew the whisky was a bad idea,' I whispered to him.

Nat took a deep breath. 'I think I want to sleep.' His eyelashes flickered against his cheeks.

'Oh no, you don't. We've got to get you to bed.' The doctor in me was in full flight now and I would make no allowance for human frailty.

With Christian in the spare bed, Alan and I managed to manhandle the semi- conscious cavalier up the stairs and into my bed. I settled him as best I could, and despite Alan's protests, I sent him home, telling him I needed the sofa to sleep on.

After a stiff gin and tonic and a catch-up on the evening news, I looked at the sofa and decided I would rather be in my bed. I slipped into bed beside my lover, placing extra pillows around his leg so I didn't accidentally kick him during the night. Entwining my fingers in his, I lay on my side watching him sleep for a long time while I tried to make sense of the events of the day and tried to think rationally about what we could about tomorrow.

I had brought a man to twentieth century England from a culture as foreign to my own as if he had come from Mars. He could not read or write modern English, he had no useful skills, no concept of working for a living. A civilized man in his own time, in this time he would be little better than a savage. On the other hand he had already proved himself adaptable. He was intelligent with a thirst for knowledge. Nat would survive, even if it meant I had to go in search of that mythical Northamptonshire forger to provide him with an identity.

Christian presented a much greater problem. I had a seriously ill child with no birth certificate and no National Health Service number. He needed to see a pediatric cardiac specialist as soon as possible and the best, and only, specialist in Northampton was Mark Westmacott.

The problems ahead of me whirled around in my head until the stress of the last few days caught up with me, and I fell into an exhausted sleep.

## �֍ 10 ֎

# FOR THE LOVE OF A CHILD

'ALICE?'

*I have tried to reach her but I only hear the echoing void of time that lies between us now. Whatever our connection, it is severed now. I am dead to my own time.*

*I stare at the ceiling as the lights from a passing motor vehicle light up the room. Jessica, poor Jessica, has not shut the curtains. I turn my head and look at the sleeping woman beside me. A lock of hair has fallen across her face. I push it back behind her and she stirs and murmurs but does not wake. She does not hear Christian crying but his distress reaches me in the dark still hours before the dawn. I close my eyes and feel the weight of the task ahead of me on my heart.*

*He is my son, my responsibility.*

*I had accepted the inevitability of my death. I never envisaged that Jessica would bring me back with her and now the future frightens me. The child and I only have each other and we must learn to make our way in this new world.*

I WOKE TO AN EMPTY BED. For a horrible moment I thought I had dreamed it all and that the events of the last few weeks were just figments of my imagination--except for the pillows in the bed and the sound of the television drifting up the stairs.

I found Nat asleep on the sofa with Christian curled in his arms, also sound asleep. How Nat had managed to get up without waking me, dress and carry the child downstairs given the state of his leg, I had no idea.

I didn't wake him, just tiptoed into the kitchen and began making coffee. The smell of eggs and bacon and coffee had the desired effect, and he straightened and twisted on the sofa to look into the kitchen.

He ran a hand through his hair, and it stood on end as he regarded me with bleary eyes.

'Good morning,' I said. 'How long have you been there?'

He shook his head. 'The child cried out in the night.' He managed a crooked smile. 'I have no talent as a nursery maid, I fear.' He pulled a face. 'He is somewhat damp.'

Our voices woke Christian, who sat bolt upright and began to cry. I extricated him from Nat's arms and dealt with the sodden nappy.

As Christian sat beside his father chewing happily on some cut up apple, I gave Nat a professional scrutiny. Beneath the stubble, he still looked pale and when he moved I noticed the grimace of pain.

I handed him a cup of coffee with his customary three sugars. 'You had enough whisky and pain killer to knock you out for months. I can't believe you heard the child cry and I didn't.' I gave him a rueful smile. 'I obviously need some training in motherhood.'

He shrugged and took my hand, turning it over before kissing the palm. 'You were exhausted. A troop of parliamentary horse riding through the bedchamber would not have woken you.'

I brought breakfast into the living room on trays. I had no idea what small boys in the seventeenth century ate for breakfast but Christian seemed quite happy to share his father's eggs and bacon and toast.

After breakfast, I changed the dressing on Nat's leg. It looked painful but seemed quite clean and there did not appear to be any signs of infection and fever. Then I gave Christian what was, apparently, his first ever bath. After some earsplitting screams, once he was in the water he quickly got used to the idea and I had more screaming as I attempted to get him out of the bathtub.

Before I dressed the child in the borrowed clothes, I checked him over, listening to his heart with my stethoscope. The obvious murmur confirmed my diagnosis. The worst would not be imminent but from the blue tinge to the boy's lips, the sooner we acted the better.

'I'm taking him in to the hospital to see the specialist this morning,' I told his father. I didn't tell Nat the specialist's name. Only Mark could do the necessary operation.

'I'm coming too.'

I gave him a withering glance and he subsided on the sofa. Even stubborn cavaliers know their limitations.

---

OUTSIDE THE HOSPITAL I knew so well, my hand tightened on Christian's and, as if sensing my tension, he began to cry. I crouched down and held him in my arms as the busy hospital moved around us.

'Okay, little guy, this is it. How about I carry you?'

I hoisted him into my arms, surprised at how light he was in comparison to a modern child of his age. His voluminous clothing had masked his frailty.

The glass doors slid open for us.

I stopped outside Mark's office and knocked. At his peremptory bidding, I poked my head around the door and smiled.

'Are you busy?'

'You know I am,' he replied. 'What do you want?'

'I was wondering if you would look at a patient for me.' Without waiting for Mark to protest I carried Christian into the office and sat him on the examining bench.

Mark rolled his eyes, checked his watch and his appointment diary. 'I've got a couple of minutes, that's all.'

Mark, for all his faults, is very good with children. Christian submitted to his poking, prodding and occasional tickling. He placed the stethoscope on the child's chest, listened for a moment, grunted and looked up at me. Knowing him as I did, the deepening frown worried me.

As I redressed the boy, Mark perched on the edge of his desk.

'You're right, Shepherd. This is one very sick little boy. If he's not operated on, his life expectancy is no more than a year, two at the most.' His voice held a somber note and I flinched at the verdict.

Now came the hard part. I gathered my courage in both hands.

'Can you do it?'

He gave a dismissive shrug. 'Book him in. You know the procedure. I'll need to get some imaging and tests done. Have the parents been told?'

'Parent. He only has his father, and yes, he knows.'

'Then I need to speak to him. Is he here?'

I shook my head. 'He's my friend Nat's son.'

Mark's expression closed over, his lips thinning with disapproval. 'Oh, I see. Well, get him to sign all the consents and we'll fit the boy in to surgery over the next couple of days.'

He sensed my hesitation. 'There's a problem, Mark.' He raised an eyebrow.

'Nat's...um...Nat has no National Health Service ID. This will have to be a private job.'

Mark's eyebrows rose. 'What do you mean he has no ID?'

'Please don't ask me questions, Mark. I've said this is a private job. My cost.'

'You know I can't operate...'

'Yes, you can.' I took a deep breath. 'Mark, I know I am presuming on our friendship...'

'Former friendship!' Mark reminded me.

'Professional friendship,' I corrected. 'What is important here is the life of this child.'

Mark shot a glance at Christian, now seated on my lap, playing with one of the drug company mannequins he had pulled off the desk.

He ran his hand through his thinning hair. 'I'll do it for the kid, Jess. Not for you or for whatever his name is.'

I rose to my feet. 'Thank you, Mark. I won't forget this.' 'Do you have the money to foot this operation?'

I nodded. 'I still have a little left over from my parents' estate.'

'And you'd blow it on someone else's child?' Mark stared at me, his lip curled in what looked like a sneer.

'He's not just anyone,' I said as I closed the door.

---

WAITING rooms of hospitals are grim places at the best of times, let alone when you have a small child undergoing surgery.

The worst thing a doctor can do is become emotionally involved with a patient, and I had complete faith in Mark and his team.

The wait was taking its toll on both of us.

I forced myself to flick through dog eared magazines filled with endless photographs and gossip about Princess Diana and her latest flame. After a cursory inspection of modern royalty, Nat lost interest and if he had not been on crutches, he would have been pacing the floor instead of tapping the toe of his shoe with the end of the crutch.

The last few days had not been easy. Nat, like most convalescent males, was not the best of patients but I found Christian took most of my time and energy. Despite my years of medical training, adjusting to life with a two-year-old, particularly an ill two-year-old, in an unfamiliar setting, presented its challenges.

Christian's father did what he could but Nat, as dislocated as his son and hampered by the injury to his leg, drew into himself and spent the day propped up on the sofa watching television. Even the crutches I borrowed for him didn't improve his mood.

The reality of Nat's situation began when I handed Nat a pen to sign the consents. As he turned it over in his hand, I sighed. He'd had no cause to write on his previous visit. A modern biro would be completely unfamiliar. He pushed the forms to one side, drew a piece of paper toward him and scratched his signature a few times. I grimaced; the florid seventeenth-century writing would raise questions. He huffed out an exasperated sigh and after some practice reduced his signature to a more acceptable basic twentieth-century scrawl.

We had a long road to travel.

'How much longer?' Nat asked, breaking the silence.

He had wanted to know what the surgery entailed so I had pulled out my text books and gone through it in detail with him. I'm not sure if it helped.

'A few more hours. It's complex surgery, Nat.' I set aside my magazine. 'Coffee?' I offered.

He shook his head.

'Is there a chapel here?' he asked. I nodded and pointed down the corridor.

He rose awkwardly to his feet and settled the crutches. 'Show me.'

I led him to the peaceful room and he sat on one of the chairs. He looked up at me and gave me a small, tight smile. 'Do you mind leaving me, Jessie?'

I shut the door and returned to the waiting room to drink another cup of warm, vaguely coffee-flavored water from the machine in the corner.

By the time Mark came out of the surgery, Nat had returned. He struggled to his feet, his face taut with expectation. Mark looked exhausted and I read the signs. It had not been as straightforward as he would have liked.

'He's through,' Mark said, 'but the damage was worse than the scans had indicated. He's a very sick little boy.' He turned to Nat. 'How in God's name did he get to this age without any doctor picking it up?'

Nat met his accusatory eyes. 'We were not living anywhere near doctors,' he replied.

'Where the hell were you living? The Amazon jungle?'

'Mark!'

He glared at me and his expression softened as he ran a hand over his eyes. 'Sorry, just a little tired. He's in recovery. Gown up, if you want to sit with him.'

How many times had I stood in the intensive care unit, just as I did now, looking down at a patient, wondering whether he would live or die, whether we had done enough? For the first time in my life, that professional concern was tinged with sheer panic. What if, after all we had been through, we lost him?

Lily French buzzed around the bed hooking up the various monitors and drips, none of which Christian would understand once he awoke. She paused in her ministrations and looked at me, hands on her hips.

'You two look terrible. Why don't you go home and get some sleep? There is nothing you can do here. I'll ring you when he wakes.'

If he wakes.

A glance at the monitors told me his condition was stable. I looked down at the tiny figure on the hospital gurney, his little face lost among the tubes. He seemed so fragile.

Nat watched me from over the top of the paper mask he wore.

'You go, Jessie. I don't want to leave him.'

I gave him a fierce look that said, '*And I'm not leaving either of you.*'

'You don't look so crash hot yourself, sunshine,' Lily glared at Nat. 'I'll go and get you a chair. You need to rest that leg.'

I followed her to fetch a jug of water. I wasn't leaving either.

Lily cocked her head and watched me as I ran the tap. 'He's the one?'

I nodded. 'Yes, that's him, Lily. Nat and I have travelled a long way together. No turning back now.'

'Well. I can see the attraction. Lucky girl.' She frowned. 'What's he done to his leg?'

I avoided her eyes. 'Just a silly accident.'

Lily gave me an appraising look before she shook her head. 'Men. Just what you need when you have to deal with a sick child.' She laid her hand on my arm, forcing me to look at her. 'Are you sure you're ready to be an instant mother, Jess?'

I smiled and nodded.

Lily picked up a chair and gave me one of her professional,

reassuring smiles. 'He'll be all right, Jess. I don't let my patients go that easily.'

Back in intensive care, I drew up a second chair, fished for Christian's small hand amidst the tentacles of tubes and set myself to wait. Across the bed, Nat kept his vigil. Neither of us spoke.

Sometime in the dark hours of the night I dozed, still holding the child's hand, my head cradled in my arms, resting on the side of the bed. An almost imperceptible tightening of his fingers, or a shift in weight, woke me and I sat up with a start.

'Nat, he's awake!'

Nat rose to his feet, his injury forgotten. He bent over his son, who looked from one to the other of us with large, fearful eyes. The change in his status on the monitors had alerted the on-shift nurse, who hustled us out of the way while she checked the machines.

She turned and smiled at us. 'Looking good. Dr. Westmacott asked me to ring him when the boy woke.'

Mark appeared within a few minutes, looking as if he had just been woken, and I felt a rush of gratitude to him. Whatever he might have felt about Nat and me, he cared enough about his tiny patient that he hadn't left the hospital.

'Hmm,' he said after he had finished his examination. I made a mental note to never to use that particular tone with a patient. 'A word, Jessie.'

He took me by the arm and steered me into the corridor.

'Is something wrong?' My voice sounded high and tight even to my own ears.

Mark glanced through the window at the bed, where Nat stood leaning over his son and talking softly to him.

'The child's not out of the woods yet but it's looking promising.'

'So? What did you want to say to me that can't be said in front of Nat?'

Mark cleared his throat. 'Jess, I'm worried about you. There's something damned peculiar about your friend. Are you sure you know what you're taking on?'

'Absolutely sure, Mark.' I laid a hand on his arm. 'Thank you for what you've done.'

He gave a gruff snort. 'Well, you're the one footing the bill.' His face softened. 'Now, as the child's doctor, I am ordering you both to go home. You're more use to me, and him, at home getting some rest.'

He stalked off down the corridor and I caught a glimpse of my reflection in the window.

One look at our faces and anyone could have seen we were done in. I bent and kissed Christian's forehead, gathered up his father and left, knowing the next twenty-four hours would be critical.

# A MAN WITH NO PAST DOES
# NOT EXIST

*Lost amidst the tubes and strange machines that emit odd noises, my little son looks like a toy, a rag doll tossed aside by an angry child. Jessica tries to reassure me and explains in detail what each machine does but her words bounce off me.*

*If I am adrift and afraid in this strange world, how will Christian manage when he wakes to a reality that no longer includes his brother, his aunt and his grandmother, everything with which he is familiar?*

*How could I have contemplated sending him here without having the courage to come with him?*

———————

BACK AT THE hospital next day, Nat and I settled ourselves in for the long wait by the child's beside. Christian mostly slept and I exhausted the supply of magazines. I wandered down to the shop to buy some new one, returning with a book for Nat.

He grimaced as he shifted his leg, reaching up to take the book from me.

'I have sat in more comfortable chairs,' he said.

I thought of the hard, oaken chairs at the Hall and doubted the truth of that statement.

'I should have a look at that leg. It needs redressing.'

He clumped along the corridor behind me until I found an empty treatment room. I peeled back the bandages, wincing in sympathy as the dressing adhered to the wound.

'Let me.' Lily stood at the door, hands on her hips.

Before I could protest she had elbowed me out of the way.

'Doctors have no idea how to dress wounds,' she told Nat, ripping the dressing off with practiced efficiency.

She peered at my handiwork and looked up at me with a frown. 'Is this a bullet wound?'

I nodded and said, 'Please say nothing, Lily. It was an accident.'

'But...' she began.

'As my friend?' I pleaded.

She glanced from one of us to the other. 'Do you know how much trouble you could be in?' She whispered in an urgent tone.

I nodded. 'My problem, not yours,' I said. 'You can close the door behind you and pretend you never saw this.'

Lily's shoulders stiffened and she sniffed. 'Well you've done a good, neat job, Dr. Shepherd. I'll just have a clean around and put on a fresh dressing.'

She smiled at the patient. 'It's only because you've such a winning smile, you know.'

Nat laid a hand on her arm. 'And I recognize a good heart when I see one.'

When Lily had finished, I looked at Nat's pale face and tight mouth and offered him a mild painkiller. He shook his head.

'I need my wits, Jessie.'

He gathered up the crutches and we returned to Christian's bedside, settling ourselves back to her vigil. Nat turned the cheap paperback over in his hands before reverentially opening the first page.

'Dinosaurs?' he asked. 'Are those the ancient beasts we saw in London?'

Jurassic Park, may have been a mistake, I thought.

From the corridor, I heard voices and my senses prickled. Rising to my feet, I parted the curtains and caught a glimpse of a blue police uniform among a gaggle of people clustered outside the door.

'Police,' I whispered.

Nat was on his feet, reaching for his crutches. 'Is this not a good thing?'

Mark pushed his way through the curtain.

'There you are,' he said, as if he had expected us to be somewhere else.

'Christian?' Nat asked, and I could see the fear on his face.

Mark glanced at the bed and shook his head. 'He's fine. No it's you, Mr. Preston, that these good people are interested in. Could I ask you to step into the corridor?'

Nat glanced at me and I shrugged. There was nothing we could do, nowhere we could run. We would just have to brazen it, whatever "it" was, out.

We were met in the corridor by not only the uniformed police officer but a young woman in a gray suit.

'Are you Nathaniel Preston?' The policeman directed his question to Nat.

Nat nodded. 'I am.'

The policeman puffed out his chest. 'Do you mind showing me some identification, sir?'

'Identification?'

'Driver's Licence? Bank book?' the policeman suggested helpfully.

Nat coughed. 'I don't have anything with me.' He glanced at me. 'We left home in a hurry this morning.'

'Mark, what's this about?' I asked.

'Mr. Westmacott has made a report to us regarding Mr. Preston's lack of proper identification,' the police officer said. 'I'm Sergeant Evans and this is Ms. Smith of the Department of Immigration. We have been looking into Mr. Westmacott's report and there are some matters we wish to discuss with Mr. Preston.'

'Mark? What have you done?' I glared at my former lover.

Mark could not meet my eyes. 'They think he may be an illegal immigrant,' he mumbled.

Nat opened his mouth but before he could speak, I put my hand on his arm. 'Nat, you don't have to say a thing.' I addressed his accusers. 'This is ridiculous. He is as English as any of us.'

Ms. Smith consulted her notebook. 'Then perhaps he can explain why he has no birth record, no NHS numbers or national ID, doesn't appear to have a bank account or a driver's license and in short, does not appear anywhere in any record in this country?'

They had done their homework.

When neither Nat nor I answered, the policeman nodded. 'I'm sorry, Mr. Preston, but I have to take you into custody.' He stepped forward, unbuckling hand cuffs from his belt. 'Until we can get this matter cleared up, you must consider yourself in detention.'

Nat laughed and held out the crutches. 'My dear sir. You can clearly see I am not capable of making a swift bid for freedom. There will be no need of manacles. I will just bid my son farewell and then you can take me.'

They all followed us into the ward, the policeman still holding out his handcuffs.

I rounded on him, a white mist of anger rising before my

eyes. 'How dare you even consider putting him in handcuffs in the presence of the child. Put them away this instant.'

Sheepishly the officer complied as Nat bent over his son.

'Be brave,' he whispered to the boy. 'I will be back as soon as I can.'

Christian who whimpered and I stroked the hair away from his anxious eyes His hand closed on mine.

'I will be back in a moment,' I said.

I left Christian in Lily's care but the child began to cry as I ushered the crowd into the hallway, where Sergeant Evans took Nat by the arm.

'This is outrageous.' I turned to the perpetrator of this tableau, my face hot with anger. 'Mark, how could you?'

Mark looked away. 'I'm sorry, Dr. Shepherd, but I have a duty.'

'A duty to your patient, who has now been deprived of his only parent at a vulnerable time.' I turned to the officials. 'What happens now?'

'We are taking Mr. Preston to Northampton police station for the time being, and then he will be moved to our detention center, where we will undertake further inquiries,' Ms. Smith replied.

'I'll get you a lawyer, Nat,' I said.

Behind us, Christian's wails echoed down the corridor, and I saw the pain in Nat's eyes but I could do nothing except watch helplessly as the policeman, followed by the little woman in the gray suit, took my lover away.

When I turned around, Mark, his work complete, had beaten a retreat. I found him in his office, writing up reports. To make my point, I slammed the door behind me and, both hands on the desk, glared down at him.

'You spineless bastard,' I said. 'This was never about Nat. It's about you and me.'

'Dr. Shepherd, Jessica, please...'

I brought my face to within inches of his. 'You spoilt little boy. When you couldn't have me anymore, you thought you would punish me by taking away the one person in the world I have ever truly loved.'

'Jessie...' He adopted a silken, soothing purr.

'Don't 'Jessie' me, Mark. I'm so disappointed in you. You were bloody brilliant in surgery. You saved that child's life and then you had to go and spoil it all with your shabby tricks.'

'You don't understand, Jess. I had no choice. I have a duty to this hospital, to the government, to report these inconsistencies. For all you know, he could have been an Irish terrorist!'

'Does he look like an Irish terrorist?'

'What do you know about him anyway?' Mark's bravado had returned.

I nearly said 'Everything, but bit my lip just in time. 'I know he's not Irish and he's not a terrorist. He is just a father who would do anything for his son,' I paused. 'And I know I love him, Mark. Whatever else there is to know about him, I have a life-time to find out.'

Mark deflated like a balloon. 'You really feel that strongly about him? There's no chance...'

I gave him what I hoped was a withering glare, straightened and said, 'No. Now I'm going to find him the best lawyer I can and then I'm going to sit with his son who needs him. Stay out of my life, Mark--mine and Nat's.'

---

I RETURNED HOME LATE in the evening, after a fruitless after-noon spent trying to get Nat released. Apparently the Depart-ment of Immigration liked to keep its suspected illegal immigrants firmly under lock and key. Not even the best efforts of my lawyer and offers of a hefty recognizance could change their minds.

I had barely sunk onto the sofa with a large whisky, when I heard a knock at the door. Muttering under my breath, I went to answer it.

'Colonel Preston.' I greeted the dapper elderly gentleman on the front door step.

'Good evening, Dr. Shepherd. I hope I haven't called at an inconvenient time?'

'Well...' I ran a hand through my hair, wondering how I could get rid of my uninvited visitor without offending him. He seemed like a nice, old fellow.

'I was wondering if I might speak with your friend, Nathaniel.'

'Ah, that's a little difficult. He's not here.'

Colonel Preston raised an eyebrow in much the same way Nathaniel did. The familiar gesture made my heart jolt.

'Can you tell me where I may find him? It's quite urgent.'

I shook my head. 'You couldn't have come at a worse time. He's in Northampton police station. Come in.' I gestured and stood aside to allow the man to enter.

I poured him a whisky and sat on the sofa. He took one of the armchairs and listened patiently while I told him of the afternoon's events.

'Oh dear,' he said. 'I feared that might happen. Indeed that was the very reason I wished to speak to him.'

I looked up. 'Whatever it is you have to say to him, you can tell me.'

He paused. 'I know who your Nathaniel Preston is.'

The breath stopped in my chest and I just stared at him before blurting out, 'What do you mean?'

A little smile played at the corners of the Colonel's lips. 'My dear, if I were to tell you that he is my great grandfather, you would think me a little mad.' He paused and his shrewd eyes narrowed. 'Or perhaps not.'

'Who do you think he is?' I asked suspiciously

'He is Colonel Nathaniel Preston who reportedly died at the battle of Chesham Bridge, is he not?'

'Maybe...'

The Colonel's moustache twitched and one eyebrow rose. 'Good, then we can stop dancing around the edges of this conversation. Of course Nathaniel has no identity because you and I both know he was not born in this century.'

I said nothing for a long, long moment.

'It's all very well us knowing that, Colonel, but it doesn't help him...or his son.'

'Ah, his son. That would be Christian?'

I nodded. 'What do you know about Christian?'

'According to the family records, he was sent to London for medical treatment and never returned. Many years later his brother went in search of some trace of his twin but with no success. It was assumed he had died. Records were not well kept.'

I cleared my throat.

'Christian's in Northampton hospital, having just undergone major heart surgery and Nat is in jail.' My voice quivered. 'I don't know what to do...'

The Colonel patted my hand. 'Now, now young lady. I agree that complicates matters somewhat but I think I have a solution to our friend's problem, if you will permit me to assist?'

## 12

# THE KEEPING OF RECORDS IN BECHUANALAND

'PAPA!'

At the sound of my son's voice I sit bolt upright, my heart beating in my chest.

'Papa...' His cry is plaintive, desperate. A cry of pain.

I run my hands through my hair, grinding my teeth in frustration. There is nothing I can do for him. Four gray walls covered in strange symbols and crude drawings and one locked door stand between us.

'Hush!' I tell him. 'I cannot come to you now. There are kind people looking after you but I will come as soon as I can.'

Through his tears I hear the words 'home' and 'Natty' and my heart constricts. The price for his life has been a heavy one.

I rise to my feet and bang on the iron door. The man in the blue uniform opens the trap door. He looks irritated by my disturbing him at this hour.

'My son is in the hospital,' I tell him. 'I need to know he is all right.'

'Listen, mate, its two o'clock in the morning. There's nothing I can do.'

*He begins to close the trap. 'Wait,' I say urgently. 'Do you have children?'*

*He hesitates. I know he does.*

*I press the advantage. 'My boy is two years old and has a problem with his heart. He has just had major surgery. I...' Here I hesitate, unsure how to put my fear into words he will understand. 'I have a bad feeling and I need to know he is all right.'*

*The man's lips tighten. 'What's his name?'*

*I give him the details he needs to know and the trap closes with a clang. I return to the hard bench that passes for a bed and wait until I hear his footsteps returning. This time the door opens.*

*'Listen, mate,' the man says and I can see the concern in his face. 'Your hunch was right. He's taken a turn for the worse and he's back in surgery.'*

*I sink back on the bench, my head in my hands and am surprised to feel his hand on my shoulder.*

*'I'll make you a cup of tea and ring again in an hour. Hopefully in the morning that lawyer of yours can get you out of here.'*

*I nod, helpless to do anything else but agree... and pray.*

---

As they led Nat into the meeting room where we'd assembled--our lawyer, the Colonel, Ms. Smith, another official from the Department of Immigration and me--my first thought was that he looked exhausted. A night in a police cell could do that to anyone, but there was more than just his unshaven chin and dark circles under his eyes. An air of desperation hung over him.

He caught my eye and ignoring everyone else in the room, asked, 'How is he?'

I didn't question how he knew that Christian's condition had worsened during the night.

Mark had rung me to ask me to come in and I had sat in on

the operation. I detected remorse in Mark's attitude. With the realization that in punishing the boy's father, he had also punished an innocent child, the fight had gone from him

'Holding his own,' I said. 'We're confident he'll come through okay.'

Nat's shoulders sagged and he rubbed a hand across his eyes as he sat on the chair beside our lawyer.

Ms. Smith looked from me to the lawyer. 'Well?'

'There has been a misunderstanding,' the lawyer said. 'Mr. Preston has been quite wrongly detained. He is a British citizen.'

'With no birth certificate,' Ms. Smith said with a curl of her lip.

I held Nat's gaze, silently pleading with him to go along with what would follow.

'Ah, but you're wrong,' the Colonel said. 'Nathaniel Preston is my son, and here is his original birth certificate.'

He opened his wallet and produced a much folded piece of paper, which he handed to Ms. Smith, who carefully unfolded it, glanced at the paper and handed it to her assistant.

'You will find it quite properly records the birth of my son, Nathaniel Edward Preston on the eighteenth of January, in 1964 in Bechuanaland,' The Colonel said

Ms. Smith retrieved the paper and sat staring at it.

'If you doubt my bona fides,' the Colonel continued, 'I am willing to submit to a DNA test that will prove our relationship. Now, release the boy immediately and let's not have any more of this nonsense.'

Ms. Smith frowned. 'I'm afraid I don't understand. If indeed Mr. Preston is your son, how is it there are no other records?'

The Colonel sighed. 'My wife and I were estranged when Nathaniel was young. My wife took up with hippies after she left me so it is not surprising there are no other records of Nathaniel's life. I cannot answer as to where she took him or what life he has led. However, he contacted me not long ago and we have been in communication.' He glanced at Nat. 'However, we had not as yet met. This is the first time I have seen him in nearly thirty years.'

Ms. Smith turned to Nat. 'Well, Mr. Preston, can you fill in how you have spent the last thirty years?'

Nat would have had no idea about hippies, but he was no fool. I could see from his face that he was trying to piece together a plausible explanation for his last thirty years of life.

I interposed. 'I doubt he can. The reason Colonel Preston and his son did not affect a reunion before now is, somewhere on his way to meet with his father he was in an accident and is suffering amnesia. He has no recollection of anything beyond three weeks ago when I came across him and his son, and took them both in.'

'Oh, really.' Ms. Smith looked disgusted. 'Do you expect me to believe that?' I didn't.

Even to my ears it sounded trite. The convenient amnesia story? Couldn't I have come up with something better?

I gave her the benefit of a small, professional smile. 'I'm a doctor. Do you want a dissertation on amnesia? You have his birth certificate, you have Colonel Preston's word and the offer of a DNA test. You can choose to believe us or not. Sometimes truth is stranger than fiction, Ms. Smith.'

The immigration official closed her folder with a snap and stood. 'Hmmm,' she said in a tone that indicated that she was not entirely convince. 'It seems I have no alternative. You are free to go, Mr. Preston.'

'An apology wouldn't be too much to ask?' the lawyer inquired with a smile. Ms. Smith cast him a disparaging look, and with her assistant trailing behind her, swept from the room.

'You don't need me anymore.' Our lawyer shuffled his papers, stuffing them into his briefcase as he stood up. He looked at Nat and held out his hand.

'Good luck, Mr. Preston.'

As the door shut behind the man, Nat looked from the Colonel to me. 'What fanciful story have you concocted? I'm not your son,' he said.

'Of course not. I know exactly who you are,' the Colonel said. 'I knew from the minute I saw you in the woods near the chapel. You are my...let me see...great grandfather by six generations.' He waved his hand at the door. 'The DNA test will prove the familial link.'

Nat looked up at me. 'What is a—'

I didn't let him finish. An explanation on genetics would take more time than we had.

'But the birth certificate?' I asked. 'That is surely genuine?'

The Colonel stiffened. His face did not betray a whisker of emotion as he said, 'Quite genuine. My son and my wife were killed in a car accident in Namibia, when young Nathaniel was only three years old. His death is not recorded in England and record keeping in Bechuanaland was never the best. Of course, the truth can be found out by someone determined enough, but I hope that won't happen. I'm sure Ms. Smith has better things to do with her time.'

'I'm sorry about your wife and son,' Nathaniel laid a hand on the Colonel's shoulder.

The Colonel stiffened beneath the unfamiliar touch of another human being.

'I am the last of the line, Nathaniel. So, you see, there are no awkward relatives who are likely to turn up and dispute your claim.'

'My claim to what?' Nat asked.

'If you are officially my son, then you are now officially my heir.'

Nat ran a hand over his eyes. 'I'm not sure I understand.'

'Who does? It is an incredible story. I can scarcely believe it myself, but here we are so it must be true,' the Colonel said

Nat looked up at his savior. 'But you believe it? How--'

The Colonel shook his head but his eyes glinted with amusement. 'It is a good story but it can wait. You need to go home, have a bath and some sleep and see to your son. When you are ready, come and see me and I will explain why it is I know who you are.'

$$ \mathclap{\text{❧} \quad 13 \quad \text{❧}} $$

## LEONARDO FLIES

*I WATCH MY SON SLEEPING. It is a miracle to see color in his face and, when he is awake, his eyes bright with life and mischief. I wish I could take him back to be with his brother and grow up at Heatherhill, strong and happy, but that door is closed to us now. We must make our way in this new world.*

*Jessica the Witch and I take one day at a time. We do not speak about tomorrow or what the future holds. There will be time enough for talk.*

———

WE STOOD on the doorstep to the gatehouse of Heatherhill Hall. Nat's fingers brushed mine but he didn't take my hand. I gave him a reassuring smile and he raised the door knocker on the neat, green painted door.

The Colonel himself answered our knock, wearing an apron incongruously emblazoned "Kiss the Cook".

'Come in, come in.' He waved a hand in the direction of the

living room. 'Make yourselves comfortable and I'll just throw the vegetables on. Then we can talk.'

Nat followed me, still limping from his wound. Every inch of wall space and the available surfaces were covered with books, paintings and knickknacks, probably salvaged from the house before it went to the National Trust. The effect should have made it look like an antique shop but it just seemed homely and pleasant.

I chose a comfortable Victorian armchair but Nat remained standing at the window, looking over the driveway toward the house that had once been his home.

The Colonel reappeared, without his apron. He poured us both gin and tonics.

'Do take a seat.' The Colonel gestured to Nat. 'You may need it.'

The three of us sat, staring at each other in awkward silence for what seemed an age.

Nat and I spoke together. 'How did you-- '

'How did I know?' The Colonel smiled. I suspected he enjoyed the mystery and intended to play it out for as long as he could. 'Let us start with family legends and the tale of the witch who appeared on the eve of the Battle of Chesham and spirited the good Colonel away.'

He looked at me. I looked at the floor.

'There is more to it than that. The Prestons are an old, well-established family and I am in possession not only of your sister Mary's diary, but also an interesting heirloom, which I shall show you later.'

'You have my sister's diary?' Nat swirled his glass so the ice chinked against the side. His casual attitude did not fool me. The fingers of his other hand clenched so hard that the knuckles showed white.

'Indeed I do, and it makes an interesting read.'

The Colonel crossed to a desk and began rummaging through the drawers. Nat looked at me, his mouth framing a question he did not have time to utter as the Colonel turned holding a small, leather bound book. He resumed his seat and flicked through the pages.

'You're probably better at reading her writing, old chap.'

Nat took the book from him and traced the embossing on the cover with his fingers. 'I gave her this book. I bought it in Italy on my travels.' He looked up at the Colonel. 'What became of my sister?'

'Ah...' The Colonel stroked his moustache. 'I'd like to be able to tell you that she married and died an old woman with a brood of grandchildren but I'm afraid she died of a fever at the age of thirty-three, unmarried and still living at Heatherhill. The man to whom she had been betrothed was killed at Naseby.'

'Oh, poor Mary,' I said, thinking of that unhappy woman, caught between her beloved Robert and her family.

Nat looked at the book in his hand turned to the page the Colonel had marked with a piece of torn newspaper.

He took a breath and began to read, '*My brother is returned to us today, hale and well. He had with him a woman, who calls herself Jessica Shepherd. I fear she is a witch and that my beloved Nathaniel has somehow been enchanted by this woman but Grandam tells me this is not so. This is Grandam's doing but what it is she knows and fears she will not tell me...*'

He skipped over a couple of pages.

'*The witch has taken my beloved Christian. Grandam says that she is a healer of great power who will take the child to London and make him well but I fear she will sacrifice him to the devil and grind his bones to powder for her evil purposes...*'

'I knew she didn't like me,' I blurted out.

Nat looked up with an amused smile and continued.

'*My direst fears are realized. Nathaniel's men have returned this morning with tales of a battle at Chesham Bridge. Nathaniel, my dearest brother, cannot be found and the men tell me he can only be dead. All they had of him was his sword. He had set charges to blow the bridge and it would seem he did not make it to safety before the bridge collapsed, he with it. It is the work of the witch. Not content with snatching dear Christian, she has taken Nathaniel from us. I gave orders for every house in Chesham to be searched but no trace of her could be found and none questioned knew of her.*'

The Colonel cleared his throat. 'I, on the other hand, had no difficulty in finding Jessica Shepherd, conveniently living in Chesham. That was the first part of the puzzle solved but there is one other thing.' He fumbled in his pocket and produced a small wooden box, which he handed to me. 'If you doubt its authenticity, you will see there is a note enclosed with it that I am certain any scholar worth their salt will validate as genuine.'

I opened the box, and resting on a red velvet cushioned interior was a single one pence piece, tarnished with age. I picked it up and squinted at the date--1994. I unfolded the paper that had been pushed into the lid and read the note aloud.

'Found under the floor boards in a bed chamber in the West Wing during demolition following fire. Sep 13 Anno Domini 1765.'

I handed the box and the note to Nathaniel. 'It must have fallen out of my handbag.' My hand rose to my mouth and I stared at Nat. 'This is what Alan meant when he talked about the dangers of affecting history.'

'Well, fortunately the course of history was not fundamentally destroyed by a one pence piece,' the Colonel remarked. 'But you can see now why I had been expecting you. I didn't know, of course, whether the time shift would be in 1994 or later. I went to the river bank last year but, of course, nothing happened. When I saw you on the path to the chapel that day,

Nathaniel, I knew for certain. Of course this year is the three hundred and fiftieth anniversary of the battle, if you like round numbers. It made much more sense.'

He smiled and sat back, his fingers laced across his stomach while we absorbed what he was telling us.

Nat spoke first. 'What do we do?'

The Colonel shook his head. 'You need do nothing. I am happy to swear to the world you are my long lost son.' He glanced at me and all humour drained from his face. 'The truth is, Nathaniel, if I may call you that, I am dying. Cancer. The doctors tell me I have six months at the most. I am the last of the Prestons, or I should have been. If for no other reason than to humor an old man, I would like to think of you as my lost son and Christian as my grandson.'

I gasped aloud as the understanding of what the Colonel was offering Nathaniel came clear to me. With Nathaniel and Christian, the Preston line would not die out. A sort of reincarnation would occur.

'Nat,' I whispered. 'He is giving you a place in this time.'

The Colonel looked around the room. 'I've not much to offer you. The family fortune is well and truly gone but there is this house and the few bits and pieces I was able to keep.' He gestured at the room. 'All yours by right.'

Nat's gaze hadn't moved from the Colonel's face.

He nodded. 'Thank you. I would be honored and I will do what is in my power to be that son to you. No one should die alone.'

---

I LAY CURLED in Nat's arms on my sofa, watching the embers of the fire I had lit on an unseasonably cold evening. An empty bottle of wine stood on the coffee table in front of us.

We had been celebrating. Tomorrow Christian would be coming home.

I had thrown myself into redecorating the spare bedroom, turning it into a room suitable for a small boy. A hitherto unknown maternal instinct had sprung up in me and I had filled the room with toys and furniture--even if he clung to Horsey as his most precious toy.

I adored the child, and in his stay in hospital, he had won the hearts of the staff.

Even Mark unbent enough to present the child with a toy car. To his credit, Mark only billed me for the bare minimum, and while he didn't exactly apologize to Nat, we took his actions as apology enough.

As I stared at the fire, the long forgotten conversation with Dame Alice crept into my memory. For the last few weeks, every fiber of my being had been centered on getting Christian well again. Now as I looked at my hearthstone, I remembered.

I sat up. 'We need Alan.'

Nat looked up at me with hazy eyes. 'Now?'

I felt excitement welling inside me. 'Yes, now. This has waited three hundred and fifty years. It can't wait any longer.'

I rang Alan and dragged Nat out to the garage, where we gathered the tools we would need. By the time Alan arrived, we had pushed the sofa back and rolled up the rug, and Nat and I sat on either side of the hearthstone, a crowbar, sacking and a spade neatly piled in front of us.

Alan looked from the hearthstone to me. 'What are you doing?'

Nat shrugged and gave Alan the sort of sympathetic glance that only two men faced with the incomprehensible whims of women can manage. 'She will not tell me. Some strange female fancy?'

I glared at him. 'We need to raise the hearthstone.'

'Why?' asked Alan.

My courage began to fail. 'It could be utter foolishness, but I need to know what's underneath it.'

---

'DIRT,' the men concluded in chorus as they stopped from their labors, sweating and panting and a full two feet down into the earth.

If the hearthstone had ever been moved since the day it had been laid, then it had been many, many years. Exasperated, I picked up the spade and dug into the dirt. Nothing.

'Keep going,' I said with false cheerfulness.

We took it in turns to excavate and I had all but given hope, when the spade hit something solid a good four feet below the surface. I gasped and looked up at the two men.

'It's here! You take over. This needs proper excavation.'

I handed the spade to Alan. As part of his studies, Alan had played around with a bit of archaeology and I didn't want to break anything important.

It seemed to take forever as Alan crouched in the hole carefully digging around the object, flicking dirt all over my living room with a trowel. He finally revealed a square object wrapped in what had once been a heavy, oiled cloth of some type. It took both men to extricate the object from the hole. They laid it on a sack on the floor.

'Well?' I said, breaking the reverential silence and addressing Nat. 'It's yours. You get to do the honors.'

'What do you mean, mine?'

'Unwrap it and see.' I could hardly contain my own excitement. No Christmas present could have been more mysterious.

The cloth wrapping disintegrated to the touch, revealing a

metal bound box of some antiquity. Nat recoiled from the box as if he had been burned.

'You recognize it?' I found it hard to keep the triumph from my voice. I too had seen this box before--in the study of Heatherhill in June, 1645.

He nodded and knelt beside it, ran his hands over the familiar surface. He touched the ornate padlock. 'We don't have the key.'

'Then we'll have to break the lock,' Alan said, hefting the crowbar in a helpful manner.

'No.' Nat shook his head. 'No need. I know where the key is.'

'What do you mean?' I asked.

He gestured at my cabinet of treasures. 'It's in there.'

He crossed to the cabinet and opened the glass door.

He lifted out a small, rusty, ornate key with the decorative fretwork and held it up. 'I recognized it on the first day and wondered about it. Now I know why it is here. Where did you find it?'

'One of the builders found it tucked behind a loose brick in the chimney,' I said. 'I just added it to the collection.'

Of course, a rusty key in a rusty lock did not turn, and Alan had to go in search of the can of lubricant. He liberally sprayed both key and lock, and after much cursing and grunting the lock yielded.

Alan and I stood back. This moment belonged to Nat.

With infinite care, Nat put his hands on the lid and lifted it to reveal the contents.

I had been expecting it to contain one particular package but he lifted out two rectangular objects wrapped in soft leather cloths. He carried them to the table and unwrapped the first to reveal Dame Alice's receipt book. He looked at me with a quizzical expression and a raised eyebrow. I shrugged.

We all held our breath as the second wrapping came away

and Nat lifted up the book of Leonardo's drawings. He closed his eyes, as if breathing in the smell of the leather.

'I never thought to see this again,' he said.

'It's not for you to keep,' I said. 'Nat, this book is worth millions of pounds. It has been left to provide you and Christian with the money you need to live in this world.'

Alan sputtered. 'It's an original?'

I nodded.

Nat set the book on the table and laid his hand on it for a long moment before he looked at me. 'Did you and my grand-mother dream this up?'

'She asked me how best to provide for you and I told her it was this book.'

'But surely gold or silver--'

'No, Nathaniel, your future is in that book.' 'But who would purchase it?'

'Museums, collectors. You have no idea what it is worth.' 'And how do we sell it?' Alan added.

'Easily. Its provenance is there in the flyleaf.' I opened the book to reveal the Preston coat of arms and the words Property of Nathaniel Preston, Esq of Heatherhill Hall. Oct 1631.

I looked from one to the other. 'It will have to be verified by experts but it clearly forms part of the Preston family estate. I suggest we ask the Colonel to put it up for auction.'

'Millions of pounds?' Nat looked at me, as if the concept had only just occurred to him. 'This book is worth that much?'

'More than enough for you and Christian to live comfortably.'

He ran a hand across his eyes before looking up at us. I felt a thrill of apprehension run down my spine. In my mind, I had planned a life with Nat and Christian. I earned enough to keep us while Nat did some sort of study that would enable him to get a job. Now the dynamic had changed. Nat could afford a home for himself and Christian, and live their lives--a life that did not rely on me.

Nat's gaze met mine and I wondered if my fear could be read on my face.

'It's real?' Alan's expression was a picture of disbelief as he crossed to the table. His eyes bulged and his mouth hung open as he turned the pages.

'This is amazing, and I must have a good look but I've got lectures tomorrow so I have to go.'

He drew himself away with such obvious reluctance that I flung my arms around him and hugged him tight. My delightful, scholar of a brother.

We saw him to the door and watched as he drove away.

Nat closed the door and drew me into his arms.

He brushed a smudge of dirt from my face and kissed me.

'It changes nothing,' he said, answering my unspoken question. 'My life is here now, with you but I would like to do one thing.'

'What is that?'

'I would like to marry you. The Colonel's days are numbered and I would that he sees us wed before he dies.' He paused. 'No, I would see us wed, Jessica my witch, for no other reason than I love you.' He lifted my hand and gently kissed it.

'You're very old fashioned.' I smiled, trying to conceal my girlish excitement at finally receiving a marriage proposal beneath a veil of twentieth-century cynicism.

'Very,' he agreed. 'Well? Do you have an answer for me?'

I bit my lip to stop the tears but nonetheless, my voice trembled as I gave him the answer, 'Colonel Nathaniel Preston, there is nothing I would like more than to wed you, if for no other reason than I love you too.'

He pulled me into the circle of his arms and bent his head, kissing me, not with the passion of first love but with the long, lingering caress of deep and abiding love that transcended time itself.

'Now, Mistress Shepherd,' he whispered, 'Let us adjourn this conversation to the bed chamber and I will demonstrate just how old fashioned I am.'

## ❧ 14 ❧

## EPILOGUE

WE MAY HAVE SNOW TONIGHT. *Through the window I can see the clouds hanging dark and gray and there is a stillness in the air that presages snowfall. Snow comes rarely to this country now and when it does, Christian runs outside and throws himself in it as if it is the most magical thing in the world. He would not think so if he had stayed in our time. There the snow is a misery and a maker of lean times.*

*The fire in the grate is only for decoration. There are heating systems through the whole house, which means it can be warm from attic to basement. The Colonel, for it is his house we now live in, spared no expense and we live comfortably.*

*The sale of my book brought us even greater riches than I could imagine and while there is no need for either Jessica or I to work, Jessica is too dedicated a doctor and loves her work too much. I would not expect otherwise of her.*

*Even though I can lead a life of leisure, there is much I want to know about this world so I have returned to learning and Alan wishes me to study history at his university. That amuses me. I would rather learn what they now call, science. In the meantime, I occupy myself orking as a gardener and a guide at the Hall. I earn no money but I feel close to my family.*

*It has interested me to learn of the fate of my descendants. My son, Nathaniel, served his master Charles the Second as I served my king. He was blessed with many children and assured the continuance of the line.*

*Of all my descendants, it is the Colonel, who gave me my life in this time and to whom I owe a debt I can never now repay, who holds my heart. As a soldier he fought with gallantry. I found his medals after his death and with Alan's help, I traced his history. He lived his life as a man of honor and integrity and I grieved at his death as I would have my father.*

*As his son, I was made a trustee of Heatherhill Hall, and at my persuasion, the trustees had my portrait reassessed and confirmed as a genuine Van Dyck. Too valuable to hang in public any more, the trustees made a copy for the Hall and one for me. It hangs above our fireplace, a reminder of my old life. I am permitted a little vanity.*

*Alan took Alice's book and made a modern translation of many of the receipts within it, which we published and sell in the gift shop at the Hall. Alice would be amused.*

*Jessica the Witch lies on the sofa, her stockinged feet beating time to the music that plays on her little music machine. Yes, I know it is called a Walkman but there are some things in this world that still defy my logic, despite the classes I take. Three hundred and fifty years of civilization means there is much to learn, but I love the knowledge it brings me.*

*Jessica will not permit me to learn to drive a motor carriage. She says I have no sense of its power. Instead I have what we call the 'Leonardo machine,' a bright green bicycle. I also keep two horses in the field that forms part of the gatehouse land and Jessica and I ride together. Or we did...*

*Her hand rests on the swell of her belly and she taps out the rhythm of the tune with her fingers to our child, who will be born in the spring.*

*She gasps and her eyes open.*

*'Oh. She kicked,' Jessica says.*

*Our daughter, for we know the child is a girl. No prescience this time, just the magic of machines that see beyond the skin.*

*Christian looks up from his game. A collection of farm animals is spread across the hearthrug, the little wooden horse he brought with him looming over them.*

*Jessica looks across at him. 'Quick, Christian,' she says. 'Come and meet your sister.'*

*He runs to her side and leans his head against her stomach. He giggles when the baby kicks.*

*'Natty says he wants a brother,' Christian says.*

*Jessica glances at me as she lays her hand on his head. 'Do you talk to Natty?' she asks.*

*He nods. 'All the time.'*

*She, like me, has heard Christian chattering to himself. Now we know, somewhere through the threads of time, the special bond that ties twins to each other still holds fast.*

*I join my family, sitting next to Jessica and lay my hand on her stomach, thinking of the child who will be born in the new year. We are agreed she will be named Alice.*

*I wonder if the blood of Nimue will flow in her veins?*

# AUTHOR'S NOTES

The village of Chesham, the Battle of Chesham Bridge and Heatherhill Hall are all figments of the writer's imagination. However the Battle of Naseby was fought on June 14, 1645. It proved to be the last great battle of the English Civil War and a comprehensive defeat of the Royalist army.

A couple of notes on dates:

--The year 1995 was chosen deliberately to predate the events of 2001 that led to the tightening of the anti-terrorism laws in Britain. It was also the three hundred and fiftieth anniversary of Naseby. The writer likes round numbers.

--In 1752, England changed from the Julian calendar to the Gregorian calendar, which meant eleven days were lost from that year--they went from September second to September fourteenth. This would mean that the third of June, 1995, would have been, in fact, May twenty-fourth, 1645. The writer felt this was probably too confusing for readers so the dates have been equalized.

On the subject of money, three pounds in 1645 was the

monetary equivalent of over four hundred pounds in modern terms, a hefty entry fee to a National Trust property.

Finally, the writer apologizes sincerely to any military re-enactors who read this book and hastens to assure them she loves military re-enactors and is sure they are not all hirsute and overweight but fine, dashing men and women. Secretly, she would love to join a re-enactment group but is geographically inconvenienced. To protect the innocent, the Civil War Association and Mortlock's Regiment are fictional and are intended to bear no relationship to any society of re-enactors, past or present.

Cover Photographs: Reproduced under license from Hot Damn Stock and Barry Wilson

# ABOUT THE AUTHOR

Alison Stuart is an award winning Australian writer of cross genre historicals with heart. Whether dueling with dashing cavaliers or wayward ghosts, her books provide a reader with a meaty plot and characters who have to strive against adversity, always with the promise of happiness together. Alison is a lapsed lawyer who has worked in the military and fire service, which may explain a predisposition to soldier heroes. She lives with her own personal hero and two needy cats and likes nothing more than a stiff gin and tonic and a walk along the sea front of her home town.

*Connect with Alison online and join her readers' group for a free book, exclusive content, contests and more at*
www.alisonstuart.com
alison@alisonstuart.com

OTHER TITLES BY ALISON STUART

**Historical Romance**

*Her Rebel Heart*

*Lord Somerton's Heir*

*And Then Mine Enemy*

**The Guardians of the Crown Series**

*By The Sword* (Book 1)

*The King's Man* (Book 2)

*Exiles' Return* (Book 3)

**Paranormal Historical Romance**

*Gather The Bones*

*Secrets In Time*

# PREVIEW - HER REBEL HEART

*Kinton Lacey Castle, Herefordshire*
*July 25, 1643*

STARTLED out of an uneasy doze by the crackle of musket fire, Deliverance sent books and papers flying as she rummaged through the detritus on the table in her search for the flint. As the candle sputtered into life, the door opened and her steward, Melchior Blakelocke, stood outlined in the doorway, holding a covered lantern.

"Are we being attacked?" Deliverance asked.

"I don't think so," Melchior replied. "In fact, I think it is our besiegers who are being attacked."

Hope sprang in Deliverance's heart. "Is it Father? Has he come to relieve us?"

She reached for the elegant French Wheelock musket her father used for hunting, running her hand over the well-polished wood of the stock. It had a kick that threatened to dislocate her shoulder every time she used it, but she took pride in her mastery of the weapon.

Outside, the entire garrison of Kinton Lacey Castle had deployed along the walls, but to her relief, the firing and shouts came from beyond the crumbling walls of the old castle. She took her now accustomed vantage point on the northern tower of the bastion gate and squinted into the darkness and confusion.

Smoke and flame from burning outbuildings lent a surreal light to the melee of men that whirled and danced in the shadows as if re-enacting some ancient pagan ceremony. Only the clash of steel instead of cymbals brought home the grim purpose of the bizarre pageant.

Two men on horseback appeared out of the smoke and cantered towards the castle. Backlit by the fires, they could have been a pair of vengeful spirits.

Her heart pounding, Deliverance raised her musket and fired, cursing in a most unladylike manner as the musket ball skimmed past the two men, taking the taller man's hat. His horse, startled by its rider's jerk of alarm, reared up depositing the soldier on the ground. For a moment he lay still, before rising to his hands and knees. Shaking his head, he rose slowly to his feet, casting an upwards glance in the direction of the castle, as he dusted off his hat and remounted his horse.

Melchior cleared his throat. "While that is excellent shooting, I think you will find they are friends not foes."

Deliverance's stomach lurched. "How can you tell?"

"They wear the orange sash of the parliamentary forces, my lady."

Deliverance leaned the musket against the wall, clenching and unclenching her hand in an effort to disguise her shaking fingers. Nausea rose in her throat. It was the first time she had fired the weapon intending to kill and she had nearly killed one of their own relieving force.

She took a deep breath, struggling to regain her composure as the two men came to a halt at the bridge over the castle's defensive ditch. Facing them were the stout oaken gates to the castle that Deliverance had shut on her foe two weeks earlier.

"Hold your fire." The man she had shot at called up to the defenders. "We are sent by Sir John Felton to relieve this castle."

Deliverance picked up her musket and drew back to a vantage point where she could see without being seen. "You answer, Melchior."

Melchior cast her a sidelong glance and stepped forward to the battlements. "Your name, sir?"

"Captain Luke Collyer."

"How do we know they've come from Father?" Deliverance prompted her steward.

"How do I know you are sent by his lordship?" Melchior demanded.

The man who had identified himself as Captain Luke Collyer produced a paper from his jacket and waved it at the wall.

"These are my orders. While I don't wish to appear churlish, sir, we have no great desire to remain outside these walls when those knaves could be back at any moment."

"What do you mean?" Melchior asked, leaning further over the ramparts.

"We appear to have seen off your besiegers for the moment." The man's voice rose to make himself heard by all on the castle wall.

Deliverance drew a sharp intake of breath as relief flooded through her. The siege was over but she still had to be careful. She put no trust in Farrington not to try and gull her in this fashion.

"Very well, Melchior, let them in, but I want every man with a weapon to have it trained on them." She tapped a fingernail on the stock of her musket. "I will meet them in the Great Hall."

"May I suggest a change of dress, madam?"

She looked down at her breeches. "Demure and ladylike?"

Melchior nodded. "Demure and ladylike."

***

"WELL, THIS IS A WARM WELCOME," Luke said, as he and his comrade, Ned Barrett, rode under the gatehouse into the court-yard beneath a bristling bank of muskets. "First I'm shot at and now this. Hardly what I would have expected."

He turned to Sergeant Hale, who had followed them in on foot. "Clear the village, Hale. Make sure none of the blackguards are left to bother us for the time being."

"Sir!" Hale saluted smartly and turned back through the castle gate.

A tall, thin man with wispy, greying hair and a lugubrious expression waited on the steps of what would have once been the castle keep, but now more closely resembled a comfortable manor house, with mullioned windows knocked through its sturdy walls. Roses grew around the stonework. A few well aimed cannonballs would reduce it to rubble.

"My lady will receive you in the Great Hall," the man announced, gesturing at the open door.

Fingering the hole in his hat, Luke, with Ned beside him, followed the man up the wide stone stairs toward the front entrance.

Despite its façade of tall walls, a tower at each corner and a solid gatehouse, even in the dark, he could see some of the walls had crumbled. The years had turned Kinton Lacey from one of Edward III's ring of stout Marches castles to a family home that would be hard to defend.

They were shown through an ornately carved wooden screen into the Great Hall. A branch of candles on the long, oak table cast a thin light in the cavernous room. In keeping with rest of the castle, it appeared to have been modernised to provide such comforts as fireplaces, glazed windows and wooden panelling. Another tribute to more peaceful times.

In the shadows of the lofty ceiling, faded, dusty standards hung from poles and rows of hooks on the walls, indicating the places where ancient weapons had once been displayed. These, Luke assumed with amusement, probably now armed the garrison.

"Are you the men who saved us?"

Both men turned back to face the screen. A woman walked toward them across the flagged floor. Luke's blood stirred as she came into the light thrown by the candles. This girl was a beauty. Soft, fair curls framed a serene oval face and azure-blue eyes held his gaze from beneath long lashes. Her perfect rose-coloured lips parted in a smile of delight as she looked from one to the other.

"Mistress Felton." Luke gave her the benefit of his most courtly bow before prodding Ned to do the same. He could see from the idiotic smile on Ned's face that he had fallen instantly in love. He just hoped Sir John Felton's assertions concerning his daughter's ability to defend her honor were not misplaced.

"You must be so brave," the young woman enthused. "There were so many of them."

"Captain Collyer?" Another woman's voice, clipped and businesslike, cut across Ned's stammered protestations of how simple the job had been.

Both men looked away from the fair-haired beauty. Another woman strode across the floor toward them.

"I see you've already met my sister, Penitence," she said as she reached them. "I am Deliverance Felton."

Luke stared. If this was Deliverance Felton, she could not have been more different from her sister. As dark as Penitence was fair, she was at least four fingers shorter, with a strong jawline, a long nose. Her saving grace were her eyes, large light blue eyes, the colour of the sky in summer. Where Penitence's hair hung in carefully coiffed curls, Deliverance's attempt at a similar style resembled bedraggled rats' tails.

"Deliverance Felton?" Luke enquired with a trace of uncertainty in his voice.

"Yes," she replied curtly, holding out her hand. "Your orders, Captain Collyer?"

Luke fumbled in his jacket, presenting her with the crumpled and stained paper.

"My orders," he said with an inclination of his head.

Deliverance Felton turned the paper over and broke the seal. A second, neatly sealed letter fell to the floor. She stooped and picked it up, turning it over to peer at the seal, before tucking the packet away in her skirts.

She looked at Luke. "I thought my father might have come himself."

Luke spread his hands. "He sends his apologies, Mistress Felton. The defence of Gloucester commands his full attention."

"How is he?" Penitence asked.

"Well," Luke replied. "Yes, very well, when I last saw him. In fine voice..." Ned's elbow pressed into his side.

Sir John Felton had only let them out of Gloucester after an hour long lecture on how to conduct themselves. They were both in disgrace. A few long nights in one of the inns and the complaints of several good burghers of Gloucester had brought them to Sir John's attention. He had judged their behaviour unfitting for the forces of the godly parliamentarians and the affronted citizenry of Gloucester and had sent them to the relief of Kinton Lacey.

"I see you have orders to reinforce the garrison here." Deliverance looked up, cutting in on his reverie. "How many men did you bring with you?"

"Forty-five," Luke replied.

Her eyes widened and the corners of her mouth turned down at the corners. "Only forty-five?"

"How many do you have in the garrison at present?" he asked, with a sense of foreboding.

"Twenty-three," she said.

Luke glanced at Ned. "Colonel Felton led us to believe the garrison numbered over fifty."

"It did," Deliverance replied. "But Father took the able-bodied men and those left behind returned to their fields and to defend their own homes, particularly once Sir Richard Farrington started to send out raiding parties."

"Sir Richard Farrington?" Ned asked.

"The local royalist commander."

"An odious man, even before the war began." Deliverance shuddered. "Always thought himself superior to us. It is his men who have been camped outside our walls for the last weeks."

Luke smiled. "You do not seem particularly worse the wear for the inconvenience."

Deliverance met his eyes with a smile of satisfaction. "That is because we were well prepared, Captain Collyer. We could withstand a siege of some months if need be."

"I see." Luke looked up at the bare walls. "And your weapons?"

She followed his gaze and a little colour stained her cheeks. "Ah...you guess rightly, Captain Collyer. We're not well armed."

"We've brought fresh arms and powder and a couple of small cannonade," Ned said.

Deliverance Felton beamed, the smile transforming her face.

"Oh, that is wonderful news." Her eyes gleamed in the candle-light. "Cannonade—"

Luke cleared his throat. "Are there other Parliamentary garrisons in the area?"

"This is a county that holds strongly for the King, Captain Collyer, but there is a small garrison held for Parliament at Byton Castle, five miles north." Deliverance sighed. "Other than that, we find ourselves in the midst of very unfriendly neighbours."

Luke considered the odds as she had presented them: Two tiny outposts of parliamentary sympathy in a county professing itself loyal to the King. Did Felton really think he could hold Kinton Lacey? This Farrington, whoever he was, would have greater resources to draw on, and would return to swat this annoying little insect of a garrison at the earliest possibility.

He looked down at Deliverance.

She watched him, with the same bright, intelligent gaze as her father.

"I have the plans for the defence of the castle in my father's library. I just haven't had the men to do the work. Of course, now you're here...Come this way gentlemen."

She set off across the hall, leaving the two men scurrying to catch up with her. At the screen, the tall man stopped them, inclining his head to Luke.

"Your sergeant tells me the town is clear of the malignants," he said.

"Excellent," Luke said, allowing himself a small instant of self satisfaction. There would be precious few such moments in the weeks to come he suspected.

Deliverance regarded him from beneath her dark fringe, her hands on her hips.

"Captain Collyer, I am impressed. With less than fifty men you have seen off a force of three times that number?"

Luke smiled and inclined his head. "It would seem so. Darkness and a little subterfuge, madam."

Deliverance turned to her man. "Melchior, I was just taking Captain Collyer and..." She looked at Ned. "I'm sorry, what was your name?"

"Ned Barrett, ma'am," Ned replied. "Your servant."

"This is Melchior Blakelocke, our steward and my second-in-command."

"Your steward is your second-in-command?" Luke asked, the ill-concealed disbelief colouring his tone.

Deliverance cast him a frowning glance of disapproval. "Melchior saw service with my father on the continent, Captain Collyer."

Luke glanced at Blakelocke and then back at his mistress. "I didn't mean to imply—" She cut him short with a wave of her hand.

"People are not always what they seem, Captain Collyer." She turned to a set of stairs, pausing to look back at the two men. "Are you coming?

HER REBEL HEART is available in ebook and print format.

# ACKNOWLEDGMENTS

I would like to thank Dr. J. Z for her medical input, my mother-in-law, PJB, for her tireless proofreading, my long suffering husband, DJB for his comments and input and my writing group for their feedback and critique along the way.

CPSIA information can be obtained
at www.ICGtesting.com
Printed in the USA
BVHW031826260819
556844BV00001B/93/P

9 780995 434202